SHHH

Shhh

THE STORY OF A CHILDHOOD

Raymond Federman

Starcherone Books   Buffalo, NY

Editor: Davis Schneiderman
Cover and Book Design: Rebecca Maslen
Proofreading: Jonathan Fronczak, Dean Gorantides, and Jason Pontillo
General Editor: Ted Pelton

Cover photo of Raymond Federman, circa 1932-33. In photo on page 249 of
members of Federman family, Raymond's mother Marguerite is standing on right.
Both courtesy of the author's family.

Excerpts from this book were previously published in *American Book Review* and *Vice*.
Starcherone Books thanks the editors of these publications, as well as Joshua Cohen
for his editorial assistance, and Steve Ansell for technical assistance.

"As Federman Used to Say" by Ted Pelton previously appeared in *The Brooklyn Rail* and
was excerpted in *American Book Review*.

First Edition

Library of Congress Cataloging-in-Publication Data

Federman, Raymond.
 Shhh : the story of a childhood / by Raymond Federman.
    p. cm.
 Transacted from the French.
 ISBN 978-0-9842133-0-6
 1. Federman, Raymond--Childhood and youth. 2. Authors, French--20th century--
Biography. 3. Jews--France--Biography. I. Title.
 PQ2666.E32Z46 2008b
 843'.914--dc22

                                2009049334

State of the Arts

NYSCA
This publication is made possible with help from taxpayers of the state of New York,
through the New York State Council for the Arts.

For Simone
The last Federman

Introduction

After the death of Raymond Federman, we always have SHHH

Davis Schneiderman

SHHH is a still point.

SHHH is a silence.

SHHH: The Story of a Childhood, Raymond Federman's last new novel, is a silence bequeathed by his mentor Samuel Beckett—even before the creator of Molloy and Malone of Hamm and Clov changed tense in 1989. The works of the two writers, Beckett expatriated to France, and Federman, a generation later, expatriated to America, share the same absurd existential laugh, but also, in *SHHH,* the same emptiness. Whereas Beckett's insularity, his cruelty, his end-of-times-in-a-jar inkblot *joie de vivre* (yes joy!) kept itself hidden within the entropic cylinder of Raymond's favorite Beckett work, *The Lost Ones* (1971), Federman's laughter-ature, his Joycean joco-seriousness, manifests in an alternate vision of literary stillness.

SHHH, in this regard, is anti-manifest destiny: it's not a movement toward the frontier, but a movement toward the story that can never be told, but now, at the end of Raymond's career, must be attempted. From his first novel, *Double or Nothing* (1971) through the "sequel" of sorts, *Take if or Leave It* (1976), through his science fiction, his poetry, his criticism, and his later works which dwell again explicitly on the story of his life told again and again—most recently *Aunt Rachel's*

Fur (2001), and *Return to Manure* (2006)—the multi-volume story of the writer Federman as the character Federman (and later Moinous and Namredef and the rest) suggests never the promise of continuity but rather the shock of recognition in the untellable. Federman, a character, introduces himself to us in *Double or Nothing* as the avant-garde writer, decades after the events of *SHHH*, involved in absurd typographical gambits.

Since then, Federman's work has largely abandoned the typographical pyrotechnics, yet has continued to reject the strain of melodramatic realism that *SHHH*'s questioning meta-narrative voice repeatedly worries might be attributed to *SHHH* by the casual reader. Rather, this is a book built on equally evasive anti-qualities—absences and omissions—an incomplete series of vignettes blown apart by the events of a history that can never be told in a straight line. Even the subtitle, "the story of a childhood," escapes the specificity of the first article. This may be "the" story—but it is only the single story of "a" childhood—one of many possible childhoods that the reader familiar with Federman's work knows he delights in articulating. It is (the character of) Federman's childhood yes, but only one version:

When they said Raymond, I heard my mother say quickly, He's not here—Federman writes in *SHHH*—and I know nothing of what happened to Simon, Marguerite, Sarah, and Jacqueline Federman, after the police truck left—Federman writes in *SHHH*—and I know that they died in the gas chambers of Auschwitz. Auschwitz that fucking word—Federman writes in *SHHH*—and Federman... Yes? What? Nothing...—Federman also writes in *SHHH*.

SHHH is not then the story of what happened to this character called

Federman before his mother pushed him into the closet on July 16, 1942, the day the Gestapo took his parents and his two sisters away and they went to the camps never to return—as it is the story of the word SHHH and what this word on the page might mean when kept like a secret stillness for a lifetime lived after these events. Perhaps it took Federman so long to write this book, a book that moves backwards in time from the story that begins with *Double or Nothing* with the protagonist(s) in America after the war, because unlike the physical and textual manipulations of the page in that wild novel, SHHH—the word itself—is not an obviously funny word.

Federman is not writing his way out of the story of his life or finally giving voice to the important events of his boyhood. Rather, in *SHHH*, Federman is stopping, quieting, creating a final swirl of mad meta-textuality just as Alice upsets the banquet table at the close of her Looking Glass adventure. The power of those two famous Lewis Carroll tales two rests not in their symbolic significance, their literary arabesques, but in their literal and visceral moments. Federman, without stopping, takes us down a rabbit hole and into a looking glass world.

Stuffing himself on noodles in *Double of Nothing*, that older Federmanian narrator is like Proust—everything moves out from the tiny closet of his childhood. The world explodes from his typewriter turned at untoward angles. Every syllable speaks in an erotic openness. The Federman of *SHHH*, younger by decades, moving back to the moment of the closet and the unrelatable swirling cacophony of his early years, professes vignettes that cannot tell us of life before *La Grande Rafle* in July 1942, but rather, only how emptying a chamber pot, spending a year in Argetan, or being asked to suck his cousin's cock become defamiliarized in reference to everything that may or may not have happened later.

Accordingly, the typed manuscript of *SHHH* is punctuated by odd spaces between paragraphs—wide gulfs in meaning—sometimes even between the start and the close of sentences that seem impossible to finish. Ted Pelton, Raymond's publisher for this book and his other Starcherone titles (*The Voice in the Closet* [new edition], *My Body in Nine Parts*, and *The Twilight of the Bums*), attributes this to technical glitches caused by Raymond's word processing program; yet rather than fully "correct" these gulfs, rather than close the spaces between sentences and paragraphs and so reunite the text, we have observed these spaces in large part when they speak to this version of Federman's story; we have respected the silences the pauses the nothing-points that mean as much in a story such as this one, as their absences, the absences of these absences, might mean in another.

During our final correspondence, during the summer of 2009, as I began work in earnest on this manuscript, Raymond offered this direction:

> Remember one thing as you read this book
> I do not write to make the reader comfortable
>
> ....
>
> Federman writes texts that impose a state of loss
> that discomforts [perhaps to the point of a certain
> boredom], (that) unsettles the reader's historical, cultural,
> psychological assumptions, the consistency of his
> tastes, values, memories, (and) brings to a crisis his
> relation with language.

He closes the note with this additional warning that a French publisher, (not Les Editions Leo Scheer, the publisher *Chut*, the pre-"transacted" rather than pre-"translated" version of this edition) wanted him to remove all the pages where the meta-textual voice, rendered in italics, interpolates and criticizes and so undoes the verisimilitude of the work. The publisher's reason: because these passages may "make the reader uncomfortable."

Accordingly, Federman exulted in telling me, and surely others, of many years ago standing outside the SUNY Buffalo office of visiting-writer Anthony Burgess, while the latter spoke to his New York publisher in heated tones and telephonic gesticulation. After pressing the receiver to the cradle, the author of deluded Alex looks pointedly at Federman and proclaims, I've done it again...I've compromised.

Whether this happened or not, of course, is far from the point of a Federman story.

Raymond never compromised. This is not to suggest that he held tight to the core values of his avant-gardism at the expense of possible fame—and that fame, when achieved in this way, entails a series of seemingly innocent but increasingly egregious concessions to mass culture. Rather, Federman's work, in its levels of pastiche, its layers of irony, and most importantly, its obsessive retelling of the same scenes the same stories the same life over the course of decades, proclaims a anti-Romantic author-centered aesthetic more directly than the most boisterous noise of many of his peers.

The work is contradictory because writing is always contradictory. Raymond understood that his writing trafficked in contradiction because there is simply no other way to tell stories.

With his death on October 6, 2009, many of us lost a dear friend, while the world lost the most raucous possible laughter and the most eloquent silence.

List closely to *SHHH*, and hear the nothingness that the character of Raymond Federman worked so long to finally unwrite.

I don't know why I told this story.
I could just as well have told another.
Perhaps some other time I'll be able to tell another.
Living souls, you will see how alike they are.

Samuel Beckett
The Expelled

Le vent se lève ! ... Il faut tenter de vivre !

Paul Valéry
Le cimetière marin

Shhh...Chut

2

SHHH

I have often told that this *shhh* was the last word I heard from my mother, on that sad July day, when the door of the closet into which my mother hid me closed.

Shhh, murmured my mother. And the thirteen first years of my life vanished into the darkness of that third floor closet. Me who was so afraid of the dark when I was a boy, me who did not dare go to the toilet alone in the courtyard because it was so dark, me who trembled with fear when I had to go down into the cellar of the house to get coal for our stove, frightened because of the dark and the rats that scuttled around, me I stayed in the darkness of that closet an entire day and an entire night, lost in incomprehension.

It took many years for me to understand what my mother meant with her *shhh*. I can still hear that word in my ear. But I always hear it in French: *chut*.

To write *shhh* falsifies what my mother meant. But since I am writing this version of my childhood in English, I have to practice hearing *shhh*.

With that shhh my mother was saying to me: If you keep quiet. If you say nothing. If you remain silent. You will survive.

Me, at 5:30 in the morning of July 16, 1942, when the French police who were doing the dirty work of the Gestapo came to arrest us because we were Jewish, therefore undesirable, my eyes still full of sleep, I did not comprehend why my mother pushed her half-naked son into the darkness of that closet after having shoved his shorts, his shirt, and his sandals into his arms.

And this *shhh* into my ear. Into my head where it has been resonating ever since.

Why me? Why not my sister Sarah, who was two years older than me, and who could have managed so much better? She was already working. In a factory. She was stronger. She was independent. Yes, why not my sister Sarah?

Me, I was just a school boy, even though I couldn't go to school and other public places any more because of the yellow star I had to wear on all my clothes. I was such a shy frightened schoolboy. And rickety on top of that.

Yes, I have often wondered why me?

Because I was the boy of the family. Because our name should be preserved. Because my mother adored me and knew that in spite of my shyness and my fear, I was stubborn enough, and enough of a dreamer, to manage alone.

Stubborn like a mule, my mother always said when she spoke of me, and always his head in the stars my poor son. My mother knew that I would survive one way or another. My mother knew.

Still, all my life I've asked myself, without ever being able to find an answer, why me, and not my sister Sarah, or both my sisters? Why me alone?

If you say nothing, if you remain quiet and silent, if you don't move, you will escape and survive, and one day you will tell what happened here. I think that's what my mother's *shhh* meant.

And it is true that the ten years that followed my stay in the closet were years of silence and solitude.

Silence and solitude during the three miserable years I spent slaving on a farm in Southern France during the German occupation. I told all that in **_Return to Manure._**

And again in silence and solitude in America—no, in loneliness, which is worse than solitude—during the first years of my exile when my native tongue was slowly fading in me, while another strange tongue was painfully taking shape in my mouth.

I once wrote a poem about this exile into silence and solitude.

Tongue

ex-
pelled
from mother
tongue
ex-
iled
in foreign
tongue
tongue-
less
he
ex-
tracts
words
from other
tongues
to
ex-
press
his speech-
lessness

I told about that exile in America in **Double or Nothing** and **Take It or Leave It.** No need to repeat all that. It's what happened before the closet that I want to relate now.

That *shhh* was not my mother's last word. It was the first word of the book my mother knew I would write some day. Yes, my mother knew who I was and what I would become.

But she also knew that before arriving where I was supposed to go, before arriving at the book, I would have to endure much, suffer much, even if I did not understand why.

That is why, after my mother closed the door on me, I heard her sob quietly.

What name to give to that terrible moment? Was it a day of separation? A day of birth? A day of salvation? Or should it be called the beginning of a long absence from myself?

That day, in the dark, I became a mythical being, like Orpheus. Not the Orpheus who sang love songs in the tunnel of death, but an Orpheus who succeeded in pulling himself out of the stone block in which he was buried alive. Later, when I came out of that hole, as I was descending the stairs on tip toes, I understood that if I turned around something inexpressible would happen. My excess of life would be unmasked as a false resurrection.

Now I realize that I have spent most of my life fearing the light that emanates from human skin. And yet, I know that death is not something that can be resolved. Death is a place you enter, like a closet. Perhaps that shriveled fetus that I was should have remained palpitating in the dark so as to bypass mortality. But that fetus had to emerge from that tomb-womb, otherwise it would never have gained the energy that comes from despair, and the ingenuity that necessity engenders.

Often afterwards, to calm the furor of my mind, I would try to go back in time and replay what took place before the closet. I tried to replay my childhood, but I could not.

I could not.

It was as though I was watching a movie playing backwards. I wanted to retrace my steps with this movie. Get back to the beginning. To the beginning of my adventure. To be a little boy again. I wanted to exorcize the meaning of absence. I wanted my life to be the reverse of resignation and acceptance. But the movie always became blurred and incoherent.

I know it's impossible to go back into the past, but I wanted to feel again what I had felt before.

Before! What a strange word. My before was something so vague, so difficult to find again, so unattainable. So ...

Phew, Federman, what's going on? This is so serious. Your readers are going to find it boring. They're going to wonder what's happening to you. If you're not starting to cultivate senility.

What! No more mad laughter, no more sexual effrontery. What's wrong with you? No more exuberant typographical gimmicks. No more scatology. No more self-reflexiveness. It's not possible. Federman is now writing agonizing realism. That's what people are going to say.

It's true that I'm on the edge of the imposture of realism in this story, and that I could easily tumble into it. But when one tells the story of one's childhood one is always on the edge of the precipice of sentimentality that makes you crumble into whining realism. That's the risk to take while telling what happened in Montrouge during my childhood.

Well, I'll go on anyway

Standing naked in the dark, holding my clothes tightly against my chest, trembling not of cold but of fear, I listened to the sound of the policemen's boots as they came up the stairs to the third floor.

The door of our apartment remained open as the policemen went in, so I heard what they said. They called out the names of the people they came to arrest: *Simon Federman, Marguerite Federman, Sarah Federman, Raymond Federman, Jacqueline Federman.* In that order.

When they said, Raymond, I heard my mother say quickly, He's not here. He's in the country on vacation. The policemen didn't say anything.

Then I heard the policemen tell my parents to take some warm clothes because they didn't know where they were going to be taken and that the journey could be long, and that it could be cold there. The policemen didn't sound mean. They weren't speaking loudly. They were just doing their job.

In the darkness of the closet on the third floor of our building, 4 Rue Louis Rolland in Montrouge, I heard all this, but I could not comprehend why my mother had locked me in the dark. It was as though I was playing hide-and-seek, but I didn't know how long I had to remain hidden before being discovered.

During the long frightening hours I spent in that darkness, not daring to open the door, slowly sinking into oblivion, I felt that my childhood was being erased. That my childhood was tumbling into ...

Federman, watch out. Control your emotions and the tone of your sentences or you're going to end up writing decadent lyricism. And you're not going to start making metaphors, you who abhor metaphors.

I'm trying, I'm trying to control myself, but it's not easy when you tell something traumatic. Something which has remained in you all your life like a hole in your stomach. Or rather a hole in your memory, since my childhood was in the process of disappearing.

Well, I'll keep trying in spite of myself.

I remained in that dark hole from 5:30 in the morning until the next morning when finally I dared come out just as the sun was rising.

The reason I didn't dare come out was because the people who lived on the main floor of our building could have caught me and taken me to the police.

They didn't like Jews. They were the ones who had denounced us when the Vichy government ordered all the Jews to declare themselves and their possessions.

I still have the official document my father received on September 7, 1941, from *Monsieur Le Procureur de la République* ordering him to appear before *Le Tribunal de Première Instance* to declare his Jewish identity and the state of his belongings. I found that document among old papers left behind in our apartment when I returned to Montrouge at the end of the war.

Because we lived in a suburb where there were not too many Jews, my father had decided not to declare us. But that didn't last long. The people in our building denounced us and after that we were forced, my parents, sisters and I, to wear the yellow star on all our clothes.

I should perhaps insert here the poem I wrote that describes the day my mother sewed the yellow star on my coat and my school uniform.

Yes, I'm going to ...

Federman, now you are going too far. You're not going to start shoving poems in the middle of your stories as you did in your other books. I'm sure that every time your readers come to one of these poems, they skip over it. And besides, your publisher is going to complain and tell you that poetry doesn't sell any more.

Well, I'll tell him that personally I make no distinction when I write between poetry and prose. And that sometimes I manage to say better what I want to say in a short poem of a few lines than with two or three pages of prose. And besides that saves paper. It's not a blockbuster I want to write here. Just the story of my childhood.

So I'll put that poem here. And hell with it.

Yellow Humiliation

my mother wept
quietly
that cold winter day
while she sewed
on all our clothes
the yellow humiliation
she said
her eyes dry now
as she straightened
on my shoulders
the soiled coat
I wore to school
just let your scarf
hang over it
this way
nobody will notice

When the police opened the front gate of our building and entered the courtyard they called out, *Federman*! And the people on the main floor opened their window and shouted, *Third floor on the left!*

Still half asleep in my bed, I saw my father and my mother rush to the window. Papa was in his pyjamas, and Maman in her nightgown. They didn't say anything, but they understood what was going on. That's when my mother pulled me out of my bed, shoved my clothes into my arms, and pushed me into the closet on the landing of the staircase.

Later I heard my parents and sisters go down the stairs with their little nomad bundles. I even heard the creaking of the gate as the police closed it, and I heard the sound of the truck's motor as it started.

That's when the story of my parents and sisters stopped. That's all I know of their story. I know nothing of what happened to them after ... after they ... I was going to say, abandoned me.

No, they did not abandon me. They hid me in that little box to preserve me. As one preserves something precious. The story of my parents and sisters closed with my mother's *shhh*. The title I have given to this book, and probably it's final word, if ever I reach the end of this story.

I know nothing of what happened to *Simon, Marguerite, Sarah*, and *Jacqueline Federman*, after the police truck left. Except the end. Yes, I know the end of their story. I know that they died in the gas chambers of Auschwitz. Auschwitz that fucking word. I have the documents that were painstakingly recorded and prove where and when they died.

You see, I even know with which convoy they left for Auschwitz. I did some research after the war. I obtained the official documents. I still have them.

According to these documents, they were deported separately on different dates.

My mother was deported first. She left from Pithiviers in convoy 14, wagon 16, on August 3rd, 1942. Eighteen days after she was arrested.

The documents specify that upon arrival at Auschwitz, on August 5th, of 52 men 22 were selected for work and received the numbers 56411 to 56432. 542 women were also selected and were given the numbers 15102 to 15267 and 15269 to 15644.

482 women were gassed upon arrival.

I don't know if my mother was among those who were selected. There were only 4 survivors of this convoy when Auschwitz was liberated in April 1945. My mother was not one of the survivors. But perhaps she managed to survive for a while. Even though she was not very tall, she was very strong. That's because of the hard work she did cleaning other people's houses and doing their laundry at the public *lavoir* de Montrouge.

My two sisters were deported together from Drancy in convoy 21, wagon 2, on August 19, 1942. They were immediately exterminated upon their arrival at Auschwitz. That's what the documents state. Except that, on these documents, the age of my sister Jacqueline is given erroneously. Jacqueline was not 15 when she was deported. She was only 12. I want to rectify that.

And yet, all my life, I have often dreamt that one of my sisters had survived, and that one day, by chance, we would find each other.

An old dream-cliché that many survivors have lugged hopelessly in their heads all their lives.

My father left Drancy in convoy 24, on August 28. He was immediately exterminated upon his arrival at Auschwitz. He had tuberculosis. One of his lungs had been removed. He spat blood all the time. I will tell later what it meant to live with a tubercular father, with a ...

Federman, if you continue like this, you'll sink into Zolaesque miserabilism.

I don't care. I have to tell the truth, even if the truth hurts. Yes, I know what my readers will say.

It's not a novel you're writing Federman, it's just plain straight-forward autobiographical writing. Or worse, what the French call autofiction.

Well, I'll tell them that they are mistaken. What I'm writing is pure fiction, because, you see, I've forgotten my entire childhood. It has been blocked in me. So I've to reinvent it, reconstruct it. And besides, as Mallarmé once put it, <u>All that is written is fictive</u>.

The blocks of words that I'm accumulating on the pages are like the bricks that are used to build a house. I'm in the process of building my childhood with these blocks of words.

So I'm going to continue accumulating, and we'll see where that'll take us.

As I was saying, before being interrupted, I know nothing of what happened between my mother's last word to me and her last breath.

I know nothing that happened to my father and my sisters, out there, in the East. I don't know how much they suffered, how hungry they were, if they were beaten, if they were cold, if they were frightened, if they saw each other, if my sisters were raped before being exterminated.

Well, everything has been told and retold about those who died in the camps. But all this has nothing to do with the story of my parents and sisters. All this is History, but not their story.

Their story? What happened after they were taken away? Nobody knows. No one can tell that story. Not even me. Except perhaps with ready-made sentences. Clichés. The story of my parents and sisters stopped when they went down the staircase. From that moment on they became absences. They were erased from history: **X-X-X-X**

But my story, I can tell it. The story of the thirteen years I spent with my parents and my sisters. My childhood.

That's what I'm going to try to tell now. And perhaps, while relating my childhood, I will also tell a bit of their story. Well, the beginning, until that moment when their story stopped. This way I'll have the beginning and the end, but nothing in the middle.

My mother was 39 years old when her story stopped. My father 37. He was two years younger. My sister Sarah was 15, Jacqueline 12.

I suppose I can say that 1942 was the year of their death. But I can also say that 1942 was the year of my rebirth. Or rather my real birth, because when my mother hid me in the closet she gave me an excess of life. And so now, more than sixty years later, I want to tell the story of my childhood. Well, I'm going to try to tell it. I'm ...

Federman, stop repeating that you're going to tell your childhood, and start telling it. You're not going to use the same old leap-frog technique again in this story—delaying and digressing all over the place.

What do you think? That I'm going to tell this story straightforward? That would be something. I've said it and repeated it many times: chronology handicaps me. I don't know how to walk the straight line. And I don't understand logic at all.

Besides, what's left of my childhood in my head are only fragments, debris, torn souvenirs for which I must now improvise a form.

OK, I'll try to tell it anyway.

This lost childhood blocked in me, except for the vague debris of souvenirs, how should it be told? How can it be found again? How to reconstruct it? Where to begin?

As I did in the preceding pages, I had to return to the closet. It is from there, from that black hole, that the story of my childhood can be told. Backward. Or at least obliquely.

But this time, instead of coming out of the closet on tip-toes, full of fear, and with a package of shit in my hands, instead of going down the stairs slowly and quietly trying to avoid the creaking steps, until the little boy that I was then started running into the street towards the enigma of his future, this time I'll come out of the closet without fear, and I'll go down the stairs resolutely to better sink into my childhood.

To better fall back into childhood, if at all possible.

To find this childhood, it was necessary to revisit the closet, and tell, once and for all, what happened later on that July day of 1942. How during the long hours the boy spent in the dark, groping at the walls with his hands, searching blindly in all the corners, he found behind a pile of old newspapers a box of sugar cubes, probably bought on the black market.

Seated on the pile of newspapers, the boy sucked pieces of sugar one after another to calm his hunger and his fear. But his fear made him want to shit. So he opened a newspaper, spread it on the floor, and crouched like an animal, holding his penis with two fingers not to wet himself, he defecated on the photos of smiling German soldiers, then he folded the newspaper into a neat package feeling the warmth and the wetness on his hands. He placed the dirty package next to the door, and the next morning, when he finally dared come out of the closet, he climbed up the ladder that led to the skylight, pushed it open, and left his bundle of excrement on the roof of the building.

Three years later, after the war, when I returned to the old house in Montrouge for the first time, I immediately went up to the skylight to see if my package of shit was still on the roof. I found nothing. Had the wind blown away my fear? Had the rain washed it away? Had the birds pecked my shitty package? One will never know. But that day I burst into laughter while asking myself these questions.

In any case, this time, it is not on tip-toes and with shit in my hands that I will emerge from the black hole. It is backward, without fear, that I will plunge into my childhood and try to imagine it.

It is true that over the years I have managed to tell, here and there, moments of that childhood—little stories, scenes dispersed in my books. I suppose now I should recycle these fragments of writing. They will help me reconstruct my childhood, they ...

Federman, you're incurable. You're not going to start reusing your old stuff. Plagiarizing yourself? Mumble the same old stories again?

Why not? After all, what I'm in the process of telling is the final chapter of the great story I've been muttering and scribbling for the past forty years. It's a piece of the whole. Of the big book I'm trying to finish now. It's the conclusion, even though that conclusion is my beginning. So I think I can allow myself to re-inscribe here some of the stories I've already told.

And after that, when I'm finished, finished with the big book, if there is still time, then I'll tell a different story. Maybe a science-fiction story. I've always wanted to write a funny sexy science-fiction novel in the style of Stanislav Lem.

But for the time being, and for the commodity and acceleration of the tale that I am in the process of telling, I think I can allow myself displaced words I've scribbled elsewhere. After all, it's part of the same story.

To begin, I have to draw the geography of the neighborhood where I spent the first thirteen years of my life, in Montrouge. A proletarian suburb, south of Paris.

First, the apartment building, 4 Rue Louis Rolland. Then the street where I played with my sisters, my cousin Salomon, and the other boys of the neighborhood. Then the adjacent streets. The boys school where I went, Rue de Bagneux. The bakery where I bought the bread and where on Sunday, if my mother had the money, I would take the chicken she had bought at the market to be roasted in the baker's oven. The meat shop, Avenue Émile Zola, and also the horse meat shop on the same avenue, and all the other shops on Rue Michelet. The open market where on Sundays I went with my mother to buy fresh vegetables, and other things. I was the one who carried *le filet*. The café Chez Marius at the corner of Rue Louis Rolland and la Route d'Orléans, next to the *patisserie*. Oh, and very importantly, the big factory across the street from our building. A tannery from which an unbearable smell emanated at all times. People who came to our neighborhood always said, *Wow does it stink here!*

I spent my entire childhood in that smelly neighborhood, totally oblivious to what was going on in the world. Oh well, I must describe it anyway.

Now the house where we lived. It was a three-story building, with a courtyard in front enclosed by walls on each side and a tall gate that opened onto the street. I vaguely remember the gate was painted green. It was an old dilapidated 19th-century building, like all the others on that street, except for one house. An elegant villa. I'll tell about it later.

I've been told that originally all the houses on our street were military barracks. They all looked exactly the same. But now many have been renovated and modernized.

(Montrouge has become *un quartier chic pour nouveaux riches*. I don't think I need to translate that.)

The staircase of the house was narrow and dark. Some of the steps were rotten and creaked. There was always a rancid smell in the staircase. The building had a very deep and scary cellar where the coal was stored, and other junk. At the top of the staircase, on the third floor, a ladder led to a little glass transom window that opened onto the roof.

The building belonged to my uncle Leon and my aunt Marie. Marie was my mother's older sister. My mother had two brothers and five sisters. I'll tell more about them later.

Leon and Marie were rich. They owned several apartment buildings in Paris. But I never knew where.

On the main floor of our building there were two small apartments. One on each side of the staircase. Each had only one room and a small kitchen. No bathroom. This is where the anti-Semites lived. We never spoke to them.

Leon had tried to get rid of them, but I think there was a law that prevented proprietors from expelling undesirable tenants.

The entire second floor was Leon and Marie's apartment. They had a dining room, a salon, two bedrooms, a kitchen, and even a bathroom. They had lots of antique furniture in their apartment. Oriental carpets. Two big buffets. Armchairs. A tall grandfather clock. Paintings on the walls, and all kinds of little knickknacks on the tables, most of them in carved ivory.

Ivory statues were in style before the war. Most of these statues were of wild African animals, all the same size, elephants, giraffes, lions, monkeys, gazelles. I was not allowed to touch these little statues, but I would spend a lot of time just looking at them whenever I went to Leon and Marie's apartment. These wild animals made me dream, and even believe, that I was in Africa chasing lions, wandering in the jungle, dying of malaria. These little animal statues made me invent stories in which I saw myself as a great adventurer.

In the dining room there were two giant Chinese vases, one on each side of the fireplace. Leon and Marie had a fireplace. In our apartment we only had a small stove, a salamander-stove in which we burned coal in the winter when my mother could afford to buy some. Sometimes, when it was very cold in the winter, my mother would beg Leon for a little coal. Later I'll tell how poor we were.

On the Chinese vases there were pictures of dragons. These dragons made me invent other wild adventures in far away places. Chinese vases were in style before the war. They must have been expensive, but even though Leon was known in the family as *un radin*, a miser, he liked to accumulate objects. Oh, they also had a phonograph, a big radio, and a piano.

My cousin Marco, their only son, took piano lessons. His real name was Salomon, but during the war he changed it to Marco, and for the rest of his life he was known only by that name. He was four years older than me. He made my life miserable when we were growing up together. I'll tell some of the mean things he did to me, and the ugly thing he once wanted me to do to him.

In my uncle and aunt's bedroom there was a huge armoire with a mirror in the center, and a bed with a big red feather quilt. My uncle Leon would hide money under the mattress. I know this because one time, when I was still very young, I saw him slide his hand under the mattress and take out a handful of large bills. He didn't notice I saw him.

The wooden floor of their apartment was always well polished. They had *une femme de ménage* who came once a week to polish the floor and the furniture. When you entered their apartment, you had to put your feet on little pieces of cloth and slide along on the shiny and slippery parquet. It was like a game for me. As if I were ice-skating. Leon would get angry and yell at me if I walked on the floor with my shoes because I neglected to put my feet on the little *patins*.

In the salon there was a leather divan with big cushions and one armchair. And also a tall oval mirror on a swiveling stand. My uncle Leon was a tailor. His atelier was downstairs in the courtyard, but he did the fitting of his clients in that salon. This way the clients could see in the mirror the suits they were trying on, and Leon could show them where he was going to adjust the pants or the jacket.

Next to the mirror stood a mannikin. Just a bust on top of a metal stem. No head. On this bust Leon put the jackets he had prepared for the fittings. The jackets still had the white basting threads all over, showing that they were not finished and could be altered if necessary. After the fittings, when the jackets *were* finished, I was the one who had to remove these white threads with a little scissors. I had to be very careful not to cut the fabric because, for sure, Leon would have killed me.

Leon had a good reputation as a tailor. Everybody in the family said that he had some very wealthy clients who came all the way to Montrouge just to have a suit made by *Léon le Tailleur*, as he was known by everyone. Some of the rich clients even came by car with a chauffeur.

My aunt Marie worked with Leon in the atelier. She did all the sewing to be done by hand, and many other things, as she sat on a little *tabouret* in front a table full of pins and needles and scissors and things she needed to do her work. Leon did the cutting of the fabric, standing in front of a tall table. He did the sewing with a foot pedal sewing machine. He also did the final pressing with a big steam iron, and the fittings with the clients.

I know all this because I spent a lot of time in their atelier doing little chores. After I finished my homework, Leon always made me do little chores instead of letting me go play in the street with the other boys. My cousin Salomon was allowed to go play in the street when he finished his homework, but not me, unless I could sneak past the window of the atelier without Leon seeing me. To go out into the street one had to pass in front of the atelier, and when Leon saw me through the window he would call out to me loud to come in and make me do something.

Humiliating little chores, like pulling the white threads from the jackets, or on my knees picking up with a little magnet the pins and needles that had fallen between the cracks of the floor planks. He kept telling me that a little *cornichon* like me should learn how to work. That's what he always called me, *cornichon*. A pickle, that's what the French call a dumb person.

Because I was so shy when I was a boy, and always daydreaming, everyone in the family thought I was mentally retarded. I never said anything. I think I was five years old when I started talking.

When someone asked me a question, I would either shrug my shoulders or shake my head as an answer. Even my mother used to say, *toujours dans la lune mon pauvre garçon*. On top of that, my nose was dripping all the time, I was undernourished, knock-kneed, and scared of everything, especially rats. Quite frankly there wasn't much hope for me. And my uncle Leon took advantage of that.

Sometimes, when my mother didn't have money to buy food for us, my aunt Marie would ask my sisters and me to come and eat with them. After the meal my uncle Leon would make me crawl under the dining room table to pick up the crumbs of bread that had fallen on the oriental carpet.

My father and mother never went to eat *chez eux*. My father didn't get along with Leon. They argued and cursed each other all the time. In fact, nobody in the family on my mother's side liked my father. They all said that he was a good-for-nothing. I'll go into that too when the time comes, and tell how they treated my father.

I was afraid of my uncle Leon. He never hit me, but he screamed at me and insulted me all the time. Everybody in the family was afraid of him. I think my aunt Marie was afraid of him too, because she did a lot of things behind his back. For instance, sometimes when my sisters and I were coming home from school, and she was in her apartment, she would quickly open the door as we came up the stairs and shove a piece of bread or a fruit into our hands, and tell us, Quick go upstairs and don't tell *Tonton Léon*.

Tonton, that's what we called Leon, even though my sisters and I didn't really like him. He was not nice, and on top of that he was a self-impressed snob. My father used to say, *Léon, c'est un nouveau riche snob*. Leon always wore a tie, whileworking in his atelier, and a suit jacket when he sat at the table to eat. He looked like the French actor Fernandel.

In **Aunt Rachel's Fur** I told how, once a week, Fernandel would come to visit the lady who lived in the fancy villa on our street. She was the only rich person in our neighborhood. So I'm not going to tell that story again. No, I'm ...

Ah, go ahead Federman, tell us again how Fernandel came every Thursday to visit that rich lady. Those who haven't read Aunt Rachel's Fur might be interested.

Okay, I'll tell Fernandel again, and after that I'll describe our crummy one-room apartment on the third floor where the five of us lived.

Fernandel was a famous actor with horse-like teeth and a huge smile that made people laugh. He was a vaudeville comedian before he became a movie star. He always played funny parts. His most famous role was that of an irascible Italian village priest called Don Camillo, at war with the communist mayor of the village. He was tall and gangling. The people in our neighborhood who had seen him when he came to visit the rich lady used to say that my uncle Leon looked like Fernandel.

That rich lady lived in a fancy private villa with a huge garden enclosed by a tall fence. She had an old gardener who was deaf. In the garden there was a statue of a naked woman. A statue of a Greek goddess. When the gardener was not working in the garden the older boys from the neighborhood would look at the statue through the fence and giggle. Everybody in the neighborhood called that lady *La Comtesse de Montrouge*. She was beautiful. She had long dark hair and very dark eyes. She wore elegant clothes, and many different hats. She had a big car with a chauffeur who came to fetch her whenever she wanted to go out.

When the children were playing in the street, and the big car would arrive, all the games stopped, and we would stare at *La Comtesse*, and she would wave to us with her gloved hand.

When I first started masturbating, I don't remember exactly how old I was, I would often see *La Comtesse* inside my closed eyes.

Please excuse the digression, but that just came to me.

Anyway, every Thursday Fernandel came to visit this beautiful lady who lived in the villa, number 15 rue Louis Rolland, just down the street from our house.

The reason we could see Fernandel when he came is because on Thursdays there was no school. In those days the children went to school all day Saturday but not on Thursday. That's why we were playing in the street when Fernandel came to visit.

As soon as his big black automobile with huge silver headlights stopped in front of the villa of *La Comtesse*, all the children would run to look at him, but never too close. Movie stars don't like to be stared at. Exactly at one o'clock, every Thursday, Fernandel would step out of the car, his hat lowered over his eyes, the collar of his coat pulled up to his ears. He looked like a spy. And he would quickly go inside the villa. He would stay until his chauffeur came back to get him exactly at five. Every Thursday, without exception. This is true. All the people who lived on our street bragged that they had seen Fernandel in person.

What did Fernandel do during these four hours in the house of this lady? Nobody knew, but the older boys would giggle and say that he came to play dominos with *La Comtesse*.

In any case, it's because people had seen Fernandel in person that they could say that my uncle Leon looked like him.

One could have realized that by going to the movies to see the Fernandel films. They were always playing in the Montrouge cinema. But to see him in person was more real. I liked Fernandel's movies, he always played the parts of a clumsy man, but I couldn't go see them very often because I didn't have money. Sometimes, like the other boys, I would sneak into the cinema without paying. Except that one day I got caught and kicked out. After that, I was too scared to try again. Especially because the man who caught me told me that the next time he catches me sneaking into the cinema he would call the police and tell my parents.

I once asked my mother why Fernandel came to visit this lady? and my mother told me that maybe they were related. Maybe she's his sister or a cousin. How can that be? I said. She's so beautiful, and Fernandel is so ugly. That means nothing, my mother said. But my sister Sarah, who was listening to what I asked, started laughing, and said to me, you're so stupid.

It was true that Fernandel, without his actor make-up, was not very good-looking. Neither was my uncle Leon who had an ugly face with big vitreous green eyes, thick lips, and a loud voice. He yelled all the time. He would argue with everybody, especially with my father.

Leon, like Fernandel in the movie when he played the priest Don Camillo, was always at war against the communists, and Leon hated my father because he was a communist. A Trotskyist.

Somehow, I think my uncle Leon liked me, even though he mocked me all the time, and treated me like a slave. Maybe he thought of himself as a father to me, since my father was not at home very often. My father was an artist. A starving artist, beside being a Trotskyist.

I'll tell more about him later.

Now I want to describe our apartment on the third floor, on the left side of the landing. It was just one room divided in two by a big heavy curtain. It's my mother who had had the idea of the curtain. This way, on one side of the curtain was the dining room, and on the other a bedroom, but the whole room was not very large. My parents slept behind the curtain, and sometimes at night we could hear them breathing heavily.

I slept on a little cot in a corner of what we called the dining room, the space on the side of the curtain where we did everything. I slept next to the window. During the night, if our green salamander-stove was lit, from my bed I would stare at its little mica windows, especially the two that were broken. They looked like the red eyes of a monster. I would watch the coal burning inside, and I invented all kinds of stories about wild fires, houses burning, and escape. I would see myself as a courageous firefighter. Many years later when I read William Blake and came across that beautiful line of his, *Fire delights in its form*, I remembered the fire inside our little pot-stove that looked like a puffy green frog.

My two sisters slept together in the kitchen on a folding cot. *Un lit-cage*. During the day it was folded with the mattress inside and pushed against a wall of the kitchen. At night, when that bed was opened, it blocked the entrance to the kitchen. Our kitchen was more like a narrow corridor than a room. It was not practical, because when my father or me had to go piss in the sink, we had to step on my sisters' bed, and they would complain, and scream, especially Sarah, the older one.

You're disgusting, the two of you, she would say. You have no manners. It stinks. Can't you go downstairs to the *cabinet* to do your dirty things?

There was no toilet in our apartment. The W.C. was downstairs in the courtyard.

In Leon and Marie's apartment, there was a place to go *faire caca et pipi*. They had a toilet installed with the bathtub. They had it installed inside one of their closets, which was quite something, because before the war, the period I am telling about, only rich people had toilets in their apartments.

But for us, my father and me, it was either the kitchen sink or the chamber pot.

Of course we had a chamber pot since my sisters and my mother couldn't use the sink. But for my father and me the chamber pot was not practical because if we peed standing up it would splash all over. So we had to crouch over the chamber pot the way my sisters and my mother did.

We also had a pail. *Un seau hygiènique*. And every morning it was my job to go empty it in the W.C. in the courtyard. Oh, did I hate doing that.

This pail was a big part of my childhood. I complained every morning when I had to carry that filthy pail downstairs to empty it. I moaned and groaned and cursed saying, It's always me who has to do this dirty work, why can't Sarah carry the pail downstairs, she's older and stronger than me, why can't she empty the pail? That's what I would whine every morning when my father shouted at me because I hadn't yet emptied the pail. Why can't Sarah do it sometimes. And it's true that my sister Sarah was stronger than me. She would kick me and punch me when we fought, and she always won. How come it's always me who has to empty that stupid pail? But my father would say that it wasn't a job for a girl, and when I kept on whining he just slapped me across the face and shouted, Get the hell out of here you lazy bum! So every morning I went down the three flights of stairs with my stinking pail.

My father was not mean, but when I did something stupid, or when I didn't do what I was supposed to do, he wouldn't hesitate to swat me.

Ah, my father, did he have a rough life. Maybe that's why he yelled all the time. I think he failed in everything, as a father, a husband, an artist, a man. He always argued with my mother, but especially with Leon. I don't know if Leon and Marie made my parents pay rent for our one room apartment upstairs, but most of the disputes had to do with money.

I'll have to tell more about my father and the rest of the family, but now I want to finish the story of our slop-pail.

As I said, every morning I went down the three flights of stairs with that filthy pail and emptied it in the toilet at the far end of the courtyard. It was heavy because during the night everybody had used it. I had to be careful not to splash myself when I emptied it into the hole in the ground in the cabinet. The toilet had no seat. It was just a hole in the ground with a place marked for your feet. Today in Paris there are still cafes with toilets like this where you have to crouch to do your thing. It's disgusting. You splash all over your legs. That's why I had to be careful when I emptied my pail, otherwise I ended up with shit all over my shoes and legs. After that I had to rinse the pail under a small brass faucet outside on the wall. In the winter the water was so cold my hands were all red and frozen when I went back upstairs. Oh, how I hated that pail, but we had to have one. There was no way we were going to go down three flights of stairs to the toilet when it was dark and cold outside. Of course, it was easier for me and my father than for my mother and sisters, because at least we could pee in the sink standing up.

My mother complained about it all the time, saying that it was not hygienic to urinate in the same place where she prepared the food, and besides, it set a bad example for the girls. My sisters would really scream when we did it in the sink. They would say, hiding their faces under the covers or covering their eyes with their hands, We're not looking, our eyes are closed. But I think that Sarah and even my little sister Jacqueline were cheating. I'm sure they were peeking at our thing through their fingers even though we were careful to hide our thing with one hand. Of course, we couldn't do *le grand besoin* in the sink, therefore the necessity of the pail and ...

Federman, do you think it's necessary for you to go on and on with those sordid details of your miserable childhood?

I have to be specific in describing the conditions of our life in France before the war so that people will understand why I had to escape from there, and what I became today. A good Californian bourgeois who spends his time telling stories and playing golf. What I am describing here is historical.

A childhood, Jean-Paul Sartre once said, is cooked in all kinds of sauces. According to him, we are all shaped by the lousy conditions of our childhood, rich or poor, happy or unhappy, doesn't matter. Or to put it another way, we are all molded by the tampering we were subjected to as children.

OK, just a few more words about the pail. It was so much a part of our lives in that little apartment.

Whenever we needed to use the pail or the chamber pot we had to hide in the kitchen, or else go behind the curtain when the others were in the other part of the room. Of course, at night we didn't have to hide since it was dark. The best place to use the pail was behind the heavy curtain that separated the dinning room from the bedroom.

As I said, it was my mother who had that idea of dividing the room in two with that curtain when my sisters and I became old enough to understand what parents sometimes do in bed when they breathe heavily.

If one of my sisters or me needed the pail during the night, we had to go get it behind the curtain near my father's side of the bed because my father used it all the time, especially to spit in. My father didn't piss very often. He had trouble pissing because he had kidney stones, like Montaigne.

It is well known that Montaigne suffered from kidney stones. He even mentions it in his essays.

My father made a terrible fuss when he had to take a leak in the middle of the night. We could hear him groaning with pain behind the curtain, and on top of that he spat blood all the time because of his tuberculosis.

One of his lungs had been removed, and in its place the doctors had put a thing in his chest like a little balloon. They called it a pneumothorax, and once a week my father had to go to the Montrouge clinic to have oxygen pumped into that balloon. To do that, the nurse used a syringe with a long needle which she plunged into his chest.

I saw how it was done because I often went with my father to the clinic to be x-rayed. My sisters too. Children of tubercular people had to have their chests x-rayed regularly.

At the end of the week, when the oxygen in his pneumothorax was running out, Papa had trouble breathing, and at night when he was asleep he would make little whistling sounds that prevented the rest of us from sleeping, and he often leaned over the pail to spit blood.

It wasn't easy to be the son of a tubercular father. The boys in school always called me *fils-de-tubard*, and none of them wanted to sit next to me in class because they were afraid to be infected. They kept saying that I had some kind of bug in me that was contagious. They called it the F-virus. I suppose because my last name begins with an F.

What a rough life my father had. He spent a good part of it in hospitals before he was erased from history at the age of thirty-seven.

My father never really worked much. He couldn't. That's why my mother had to clean other people's houses and do their laundry so she could feed her children.

Ah, all this is so sad! I'll have to tell something funny soon otherwise I'll get depressed, and the readers too.

I imagine the only pleasure my mother must have had in her miserable life is when she was cleaning the apartment of the rich people in the fancy neighborhoods. During the long hours she spent on her knees scrubbing floors, she would say to herself, It's beautiful here. I feel a bit like I am in my house when I clean here. And while dusting the antique furniture and the rare objects, while making the beds, washing the pots and pans, carefully pressing the collar of Monsieur's shirts making sure not to make false pleats, she would say to herself, What beautiful things these people have, while absently contemplating her chapped hands.

As for my father, he was a strange man. An incurable foreigner. Not only a tubercular artist, but also a gambler, and a womanizer. Well, that's what all my aunts and uncles on my mother's side said about him—that he had mistresses. And I believe that, because my father, in spite of his tuberculosis, was very handsome. He had brown curly hair always well groomed. Eyes grey like a stormy sky. Eyes that were forever looking elsewhere, far away. He was elegant. Always well dressed. Even though we were poor, he wore good suits. Even silk shirts and silk ties. His shoes were well polished. I was the one who polished them. Papa would give me one *sou* every time I polished his shoes. I kept the polish and the brush under my cot with my other things.

Sometimes when my father was not home, I would put on one of his felt hats. He had several of them. The hat was, of course, too big for my head, and would fall over my eyes, and my sisters would laugh at me. Ah, my sisters! What a big hole of absence they dug in me. I've never been able to fill that hole because I have so few souvenirs of what we did together, of what we said to each other. No memory of words that passed between us. I am sure we played games together. We argued and fought, like all brothers and sisters do. Especially me with my sister Sarah. Sarah and me, we didn't get along too well. She thought of herself superior because she was older. She liked to be left alone. She spent much of her time reading, especially the books of *La Comtesse de Ségur*. She had several of them. I don't know how she managed to get them. There was one she read and reread constantly, *Les malheurs de Sophie*.

My mother often told the story of how a few months after I was born, one sunny summer day she had put my crib outside in the courtyard, and sat in the shade knitting me a warm sweater for the winter, she hadn't noticed that my sister Sarah, who was then two years old, had toppled my crib upside down, and I was underneath crying, flat on my face, my nose pressed against the ground. My mother would say that my sister Sarah had done that because she didn't want a little brother.

I preferred to play with my sister Jacqueline. She was shy like me, but not as much. She giggled all the time. She was Papa's favorite. *Sa petite chouchou*. Sometimes, when my father was in a good mood, he would ask her to dance, and Jacqueline would do some pirouettes, then my father would kiss her and tell her how beautiful she was.

Jacqueline always said that she wanted to become a ballerina. It's true that she was beautiful with her long curly hair. She looked like Papa. Same grey eyes. Sarah and me, we resembled Maman who had big dark eyes always full of tears.

When Papa was in a good mood we were all happy. Even my mother. He was so unpredictable. To tell the truth, I barely knew him.

He spoke six languages. Polish, Russian, German, Czech, French, and Yiddish. I know this because the men with whom he played cards in the cafes spoke all these languages. That's something else I'll have to tell, my father's political activities, and his other activities.

Sometimes my father didn't come home for several nights, and my sisters and I would ask Maman, Where is Papa? And Maman would say, Shhh, Papa is working. And we would say, He works during the night? Maman would explain. He likes to work at night. I never understood what kind of work Papa did, but I could tell Maman didn't want to answer any more questions.

When Papa returned from one of his absences, he would always tell us a story. A fabulous story of political intrigue. A revolution. The way he told it, it was like a great adventure. Then he would say to us, Wait till the day comes when we'll all go back to Russia, you'll see how beautiful it will be. Sometimes he would sing a song in Russian. He would also sing the International in French and in Russian, and my sisters and I would sing along with him. That's how I learned the words of that song, which I still remember today.

When we sang the International with Papa, Maman would say, *Shhh*, not so loud. Tonton Léon is going to hear, and he'll make a fuss.

My sisters and I loved when Papa told us stories, but he only told what he did during the day, never what he did during the night when he didn't come home.

My mother's sisters would tell her that her husband was sleeping with his *courveh*. They would say that in Yiddish, so I didn't really understand what that word meant. The only Yiddish words I knew were the insults Papa and Leon would shout at each other when they had an argument, or when Papa was cursing Maman.

That's how I learned Yiddish insults when I was a boy. I still remember a few of these, but I can only say them. I don't know how to spell them.

For instance this one, *Geh in Drerde*, which I write the way I hear it when I say it. Literally translated I think it means, Go get buried, or disappear into the earth. And this one also, *Wer verblunjet mit ein sibelles in dem toochess*. Which means, more or less, Go get flushed away with an onion up your ass.

So when my mother's sisters told Maman in Yiddish what Papa was doing when he didn't come home, my sisters and I would ask Maman, Where is Papa tonight? What is he doing? Why didn't he come home? And Maman would say, *Chut, geh schlafen*. And she would kiss us. And my sisters and I would ask, after Maman had turned off the light, Isn't Papa scared all alone in the dark? And Maman would say, *Schlaf mein kinder*.

I am now convinced that my father had mistresses. In fact, I found proof. But before telling how I found out that my father was unfaithful to my mother, I have to do a long detour to explain how I got the proof. First, I have to return to the description of our apartment.

We didn't have much furniture in our little apartment. In the kitchen there was a small rusty gas stove on a counter, and above it a wall cabinet in which the dishes were stored. There was a sink, but no hot water. To wash our clothes my mother would heat the water on the stove. She also had to warm water to bathe us. My sisters' folding cot was stored against the wall in the kitchen that faced the window. Because we didn't have a refrigerator, in the winter my mother would keep milk and meat outside on the window ledge.

Oh, I mustn't forget *la cuvette*. The big wash-basin in which my mother would bathe me when I was little. Maybe this is a good place to put the poem I wrote about that.

The Wash-basin

my fondest pleasure
when I was a little boy
was when my mother
gave me a bath on sundays

naked I stood in the wash-basin
in the middle of the kitchen and
abandoned myself to the soft hands
of my mother who hummed dreamily
while scrubbing my frail white body

when the water became too cold
and I was starting to shiver
my mother would wrap a towel
around me and rub me hard all over

after that she would hold me tight
against her and after she finished
squeezing me she would say
go get dressed quickly now

I think it made my mother happy
to give me a bath in the little basin
while singing love songs to herself
I could see that in her big black eyes

In the room which was both dining room and bedroom, there was an old buffet in which mother stored all our possessions. Next to it was my father's old hand-cranked phonograph with its big speaker, and near the window our green salamander-stove with its little mica windows. As I mentioned before, two of them were broken, so that you could see the fire burning inside the stove which made me dream of wild adventures. When my mother would see me staring at the stove, she would say, My little Raymond is lost in the clouds again.

That was my mother's favorite expression when I was day-dreaming. Years later, when I started reading my horoscope every day, as I still do, the best description that was given for a Taurus was, someone who lives with his feet on the ground and his head in the clouds. Yes, of course, I'm a Taurus. I was born on May 15. A Sunday. My mother often said that I was lazy because I was born on a Sunday. But I don't think

...

Federman, now you're really exaggerating. You tell too many things at the same time. Your readers are going to get lost in all these stories within stories. Can't you finish one story before starting another one? With all these detours and interruptions, for sure you'll forget half of what you promise to tell us.

I cannot write any other way. When I start telling something that happened during my childhood, all kinds of other things come bursting into my head, so I have to mention them otherwise I'll really forget them.

So let me go on digressing.

I was in the middle of describing our apartment.

Across from the phonograph was my father's old shabby armchair. Some of the stuffing was coming out of the cover. Papa would sit in it to read his newspapers or to listen to music. He loved music. Especially opera. His favorite was Tosca. When he wanted to listen to music, he would ask me to put the disk on the phonograph, and while I was rewinding it with the little crank, each time Papa would tell me the story of Tosca, and how she hurled herself to her death from the parapet of a fortress when she discovered that her lover Mario had been killed.

One time, my father took me with him to see Tosca at the Paris Opéra, *Place de l'Opéra*. I fell asleep during the first act. But I was happy that day to have gone out with my father. That didn't happen often. Except once in a while, he would take me with him to one of the political demonstrations, *Place de la République*. That too, I'll have to tell. How, when I was a boy, on May Day, I sang the International with my father and his communist friends.

The day my father took me to the opera it was very cold. In winter my father wore a heavy dark blue overcoat made of a thick fabric. As we walked from the métro to the opera house, Papa held one of my hands inside the pocket of his coat to warm it. I didn't have gloves. I was so happy that day.

Since I am talking about my father's passion for music, I should perhaps insert here the piece I once wrote about his favorite song, "Ramona". It'll give an idea of what type of man my father was, and ...

Federman, one of these days you're going to get lost in your own stories, and you won't know how to get back to the real world.

I've managed quite well until now with my leap-frog technique.

Besides, as I've often said, the real world, it's a nice place to visit, but I wouldn't want to live there permanently.

RAMONA

My father's favorite song was "Ramona." It goes like this, *Ramona je t'aimerai toute la vie, Ramona je t'aimerai toute la vie* ... I only know the words in French. But I think that song also exists in English.

My father, the dreamer, the starving romantic, the Trotskyist, the gambler, the womanizer, the *Brudny yd* as he was often called, my tubercular father, who never achieved his vocation, while listening to *Ramona* on the scratched disk playing on our old dusty phonograph with the big speaker and the little crank, my father, Papa, *Tate*, was dreaming. I could tell he was dreaming.

Sometimes towards the end of the song, when the phonograph was unwinding and needed to be cranked again, the voice of the singer would whine into distortions, and the song would become so slow, so sad.

I never knew who was singing the recording of "Ramona" that my father loved so much. It was a woman, a young woman, I think, with a beautiful deep sad raspy voice. She died young. She died of tuberculosis. That's what my father told me one day. That's all I know about her. I don't even know her name, or perhaps I knew it once but have forgotten it. But when I listened to "Ramona" with Papa, I would feel tenderness towards her. Yes, tenderness. Not passion. I was too young then to know what passion was.

Papa, I'm sure, knew what passion was. He was a passionate man. He loved women. *Il était coureur de femmes*. That's what all my aunts and uncles always said about him, *un coureur de femmes*, but also *un fainéant, un rien-du-tout. Papa.*

So what. Maybe that's what he left me when he changed tense. His passion. His passion for women. For love. For sex? Look, it's not because I am writing about my father that I have to become prudish.

Yes, even me, while listening to the sad voice of the singer singing Ramona *je t'aimerai toute la vie* ... I would feel tenderness for her, and I would imagine her being *petite et fragile*, with very long black hair and very long eyelashes. That's all I could imagine about her then. Today I could imagine her much better if I could listen to her sing *Ramona*. Today I know how to imagine a beautiful woman.

When papa listened to "Ramona" there was dreaming in his eyes, I could see that, and I know he was dreaming about his failed vocation. And probably also about his failed loves. When papa listened to Ramona, sitting in his old broken down armchair, facing the phonograph, I could tell he was making up stories about how he could have been great if ...

Ah! yes, if ...

I could see it in his eyes, but I could also feel it in his fingers, in his fingernails gently scratching my back. As I sat on the floor next to his armchair, I would say to him, *Papa gratte-moi le dos, s'il te plaît, ça me gratte là, près de l'omoplate gauche*, and my father would scratch my back. We had studied human anatomy in school, that's why I could tell my father to scratch my left clavicle because it itched.

I could feel he was dreaming in the way his fingers moved slowly on my back. He was dreaming of the great works of art he would have liked to have created, but never did.

Not because he was lazy, as my aunts and uncles said he was, and not because he was sick all the time. But because he was not ready yet. The tense changed too soon for him. I am sure he would have created something immortal, if he had been given the time. I could feel it in his fingers. Papa had beautiful hands, with long fingers.

Deep inside he knew he had failed, failed to achieve what was inscribed in him, by his father, or some remote ancestor.

All the others before him, his father, grand-father, great-grand-father, and all those who preceded them probably failed each in their own way. Except that, it is said, that there was one Federman who, way back in the 16th century, was a famous conquistador who became very rich in the new world. But he was a mean bastard, and as the story goes, the ship which was bringing him back to Europe sank in the ocean, and all the treasures he had accumulated disappeared forever.

I once wrote a poem about my father's ancestors. I'll put it here, for whatever it's worth. It's called ...

BEFORE THAT

Some say, can say: my father was a farmer,
and his father before him, and his father
before that. We are of the earth.

Others say, can say: my father was a builder,
and his father before him, and his father
before that. We are of the stone.

And others can say: my father was a sailor,
and his father before him, and his father
before that. We are of the water.

They have been farmers, builders, sailors,
no doubt, since the time earth, stone, water
entered into the lives of men, and still are.

I am a writer, but I cannot say: my father
was a writer, nor his father before him,
nor his father before that. I have no antecedent.

My father, and his father before him, and his father
before that were neither of the earth, nor of the stone,
nor of the water. The world was indifferent to them.

I write, perhaps, so that one day my children can say:
my father was a writer, the first in our family.
We are now of the word. We are inscribed in the world.

I feel I could write on the earth, on the stone.
It seems to me that I could even write on water.
I write to establish an antecedent for my children.

Five thousand years without writing in my family,
what can I do against this force which presses
behind me? Say that I write to fill this void?

Say, I suppose, that of my father I cannot say anything,
except what I have invented to fill the immense gap
of his absence, and of his erasure from history.

No, I am wrong, you see, because I can say: my father
was a wanderer, he came from nowhere and went nowhere.
He came without earth, stone, water, and he went wordless.

While contemplating his failures, and absentmindedly scratching my back, my father was perhaps thinking that his son, I mean me, would someday achieve what he had failed to achieve. And so, aware that his tuberculosis might soon kill him, or that some unforgivable enormity would erase him from history, Papa with his hand on my back would try to make me feel this yearning for greatness. With the tips of his fingers he would try to transmit his dreams into my body, into my skin, my flesh, my bones.

Lost in his reveries, as I was slowly dozing off under the gentle touch of his hand, Papa would ... ah, shit how shall I say it ...? He would give me my inheritance. His dreams. That's all he gave me.

The other day, while taking a shower, I surprised myself humming *Ramonaaaa je t'aimeraiiiii toute la vieeee* ... letting my voice drag the words into the soapy water.

Now back to the description of our apartment. In the middle of the dining room stood a big table and five chairs, since we were five living in that room. And against the wall, near the window, the cot on which I slept.

That cot, even when it became a bit too small for my growing body, was my private domain.

I kept my tin soldiers and my stamp collection under that bed. I mostly collected stamps from the French colonies because they were big and beautiful, with pictures of people of different colors and wild animals. My stamp collection made me want to explore these far-away places. I would imagine myself being a daring adventurer, or a soldier in *La légion étrangère*. I had one stamp from Senegal that I particularly loved because it was triangular. I'd gotten it from one of the older boys at school. I gave him two cigarettes for that stamp. Two cigarettes I'd stolen from my father's pack.

Under my bed I also kept my marbles and my knuckle-bones. I liked playing these games in the street with the other boys my age, even though I rarely won. But the most important things I kept under my bed were my Jules Verne books. Ah, Jules Verne! Sometimes, during the night, when my parents were asleep, I would read one of Jules Verne's books under the blankets with a little flashlight.

My favorite was *Michel Strogoff*. I kept rereading it. I wanted to be like Michel Strogoff. I wanted to have my eyes burned like his by the inflamed sword of a Russian Cossack of the Tzar's army. I also wanted to go around the world in eighty days, and to the moon, and to the center of the earth, and to the bottom of the sea. I had all the Jules Verne, but also other adventure books. Especially cloak-and-dagger novels. My parents could not afford to buy me these books, so I would have to wait until my cousin Salomon had finished reading his so he could give them to me. They were not always in good condition, but still I wanted them. Salomon didn't really care to keep his books. He always got everything he wanted. The aunts and uncles would spoil him just because he was the first of all the cousins.

He also had a lot of comic books, but he was not allowed to read them until he finished his homework and his piano lessons. If Leon caught him reading a comic book before he was finished, Leon would really get angry.

Sometimes, when Salomon was upstairs doing his homework, and his parents were working downstairs in the atelier, he would send me to buy comic books for him. I had to hide them inside my pants to bring them back upstairs.

To go up into the house, I had to pass in front of Leon's atelier, and if my uncle saw me trying to sneak by the window, he would shout, Come here, you little coward and let me see what you're hiding in your pants. Leon had caught me several times with comic books hidden inside my pants against my stomach, and each time I had to explain that it was Salomon who sent me to get them. I would go buy those comic books for my cousin because I knew that when he'd be finished reading them I would get them.

So I stood piteously in front of my uncle Leon while he shoved his hand inside my pants and pulled out *Les Pieds-Nickelés* or *Mandrake le magicien* or *Tarzan* or *Tintin,* and many others like that.

Leon would throw the comics into the garbage can, and then he would step out into the courtyard and call out to Salomon to come down, and when my cousin came into the atelier Leon would slap him hard across the face. There was such anger in Leon's eyes, it frightened me. But he never hit me. It was always Salomon who got it because of the comic books.

I'll tell you more about my cousin Salomon when I am finished describing our apartment.

It's in my cot that I masturbated for the first time. And often after that. I'll have to tell that too later. Sorry to mention it, but it was something I did when I was growing up. It was part of my childhood. And I suppose part of every boy's childhood.

Behind the curtain where my parents slept, there was a nightstand on my father's side of the bed on which he kept his personal things. His medicine, his wallet, his watch, his cigarettes. Even though he had tuberculosis, my father smoked all the time. *Gitanes* without filters. In those days, cigarettes didn't have filters. Sometimes my father would send me to the bureau de tabac at the corner of our street to buy his cigarettes.

On the side of the bed where my mother slept, there was a small, narrow closet in which our clothes were stored and where my parents kept their private papers in cardboard boxes.

I made this long descriptive detour of our apartment just to arrive at this closet which was not the closet into which my mother hid me.

That closet was on the landing. In it we kept things we didn't need every day.

When I returned to Montrouge at the end of the war, after the three miserable years I spent on the farm in Southern France, I discovered that everything in our apartment had been stolen. Everything. Probably by the neighbors, though they claimed that it was the Germans who took everything. I never believed that.

What was curious is that in Leon and Marie's apartment everything remained just like before. I mean, before they left for the free zone, a few days before the big round-up of the Jews. Every piece of furniture was in place.

I learned later it was Marius, from the corner café, who warned Leon that all the Jews in Paris and in the suburbs were going to be arrested. Marius' brother-in-law was a *gendarme*, and he is the one who told him when *La Grande Rafle* would take place.

The Jews who had money were able to escape to the free zone by paying the *passeurs*, as they were known. These were people who made deals with the Germans so they could sneak Jews across the line of demarcation. They would split the money they got with the Germans. Sometimes, they would get more than money. They would force the frightened Jews to give them the jewelry they had taken with them.

That's where all my mother's brothers and sisters went. To the free zone. They all had money, and that's why they all survived.

It has not been said enough that mostly the poor Jews were deported and died in the camps. Those who could not afford a train ticket to get away. Those who were abandoned by their families, as my parents were.

A few days before the great round-up, aunt Marie came up to our apartment, and said to my mother, Take the children and come with us, and leave him behind, your lazy good-for-nothing husband.

My father was not home that day, when aunt Marie said that to my mother. But my sisters and I heard what she said, *Prends les gosses et viens avec nous, et laisse-le lui*. And we saw how my mother spat in her sister's face as she burst into tears.

Lui, him, that was my father, whom everybody in the family hated.

I witnessed that scene. It has remained inscribed in me.

Well, enough of that. I've already told that ugly scene in **Aunt Rachel's Fur**. What I wanted to say, is that in Leon and Marie's apartment everything was there when they returned at the end of the war. They payed someone to watch over their possessions. Probably Marius and his brother-in-law.

Marius and Leon were always making deals. Marius would buy food from the black market for my uncle, and Leon would make pants for him for free. Marius was known in the neighborhood as the king of the black market. He could get anything that was rationed. Anything. Eggs, meat, soap, sugar, chocolate, perfume, silk stockings, anything that could no longer be found in grocery stores or the department stores during the German occupation.

I suppose that's why nothing was stolen from Leon and Marie's apartment. But in our place everything had been pillaged.

The lock on the door of our apartment was broken, and inside it was completely empty, except for a broken chair shoved into a corner of the room next to the old musty mattress of my parents' bed. Everything else had disappeared. The buffet, my father's phonograph, his armchair, the stove, my sister's folding bed. Everything. Even the chamber pot and the hygienic pail. Even my sisters' dolls and my tin soldiers. And my stamp collection too. And all my Jules Verne.

I remember how I stood in the middle of this emptiness, trying to imagine how it was when we were still living there, even though it was small, it was our home. The floor creaked as I walked to the kitchen. My steps left marks in the dust on the floor. I looked in the kitchen. It was completely empty. I looked into the small closet. On the floor there was a pile of rags. Torn old clothes that were probably found useless by those who came to take away our possessions. But in the small bedroom closet I found a cardboard box full of old torn and yellowed letters and papers, and a few photos. Family photos.

These old rags, these documents and these photos, that's all that was left of my family. My inheritance.

I sat on the floor and one by one I took out the old papers and photographs from that box. Most of the papers were in such bad condition they were falling apart. The one thing I did find that was still in good condition was a *livret de la caisse d'épargne de Montrouge* made out to me.

I'll tell later how I got this saving's account booklet, and how I succeeded in collecting the money. It's a very funny story. But first …

Do you know Federman what you should do before going on? You should make a list of all the stories you promised to tell us. This way, you won't forget.

Good idea. A list like that will wet the potential readers' mouths, if I may allow myself a liquid metaphor, and this way they'll want to continue reading. It will keep them in suspense.

Okay, I'll make a list of these stories before revealing what I found in that box in the bedroom closet that convinced me that my father was probably unfaithful.

List of scenes of my childhood to be written.

1. Scene describing how my uncle Leon planted a tree in the courtyard of our building.

2. Scene describing the savings account booklet I found in the box in the small closet, and how I succeeded in collecting the money when I returned to France for the first time, after ten years in America.

3. Scene describing how I once stole a ring in a department store.

4. Scene describing how after school with the other boys from our neighborhood we played soccer in the street, not with a soccer ball, but with a little wooden palette that would demolish our shoes, which made my mother very unhappy because she could not afford to buy me new shoes. In fact, concerning shoes, I had to wait until my cousin Salomon's shoes became too small for him, to be handed down to me by my aunt Marie. But these used shoes were already too small for me because, even though I was younger than my cousin Salomon, my feet were bigger than his. I suppose, there is nothing much more that can be said about that.

5. Scene describing how mean one of the teachers in school had been, and how he would throw a metal ruler at us if we spoke in class, and how when he came back from the war he had lost a leg, and he was not as mean, and how we would laugh when we saw him walk with only one leg and his crutches. We would call him *le boiteux*.

6. Scene describing how one day when I went to my cousin Salomon, to ask him to help me with my algebra homework, he tried to force me to suck his cock.

7. Scene describing how, one day, when I was playing doctor with my sister Jacqueline, we almost got caught by my mother. It was the day war was declared.

8. Scene describing how my cousin Salomon, one day, when we were playing in the street in front of our house, tied me with a rope down in a ditch some workers had dug in the street, and how he shoved a handkerchief in my mouth so I couldn't shout, and how I couldn't untie myself and answer my mother when she called out from the window of our apartment for me to come home because it was starting to get dark.

9. Scene describing the Exodus at the beginning of the war, and how all the people left Paris as the German soldiers approached the city, and how my parents and sisters and me, we walked carrying suitcases on the roads of Normandy with thousands of other people, and how we saw French soldiers in retreat, and also how we saw dead people when the enemy airplanes fired at us with machine guns.

10. Scene describing how we wandered for days on the roads of Normandy, and how when we arrived in Argentan the Germans were already there, and how I was impressed with their uniforms, especially the officers' uniforms.

11. Scene describing the house in Argentan in which the Germans put us, and where we stayed for almost a year, and how my mother would fix the German soldier's uniforms, do their laundry, press their

shirts, and how my father would get stuff from the black market for the German soldiers, and how they would bring us food, and how in the evening German soldiers came to our house to discuss politics with my father, and how I would go to the store to buy bottles of beer for the German soldiers, and how before leaving late in the evening, they would all raise their left fist and together with my father they would sing the International, and me too, I would sing with them in a soft voice. The German soldiers who came to our house were all Communists, like my father. My father explained to me that the best place for German Communists to hide was in the army.

12. Scene demonstrating how verisimilitude often becomes improbable when one tells a story.

13. Scene describing the Argentan *Lycée* where I got my *certificat d'études*, and how the boys used to fight with chestnuts that fell from the trees that surrounded the school playground, and how I would also throw chestnuts at them.

14. Scene describing how, during the very cold winter we spent in Argentan, one day the German soldiers who came to discuss politics with my father unloaded a whole truck of coal in front of our house, and how all the neighbors were saying that we were collaborators.

15. Scene describing how the children in Argentan played on the big square in front of the church where the Germans had piled up the gas masks and the rifles and the helmets abandoned by the retreating French army.

16. Explain how, when the war started, all the people in the cities had to carry a gas mask everywhere they went. Even the children.

17. Scene describing the night when the tannery in front of our house caught fire, and how all the people in our street had to be evacuated, and how the firemen fought the fire, and how I wished our house would also burn so we could move away from this neighborhood.

18. Describe how, after the burnt factory had been completely demolished, we had a view of the whole city from the window of our apartment on the third floor.

19. Describe the wasteland—*La Zone*, as it was called—between Porte D'Orléans and Montrouge, and how the Arabs from the colonies, we called them *Les Sidis*, slept in this no-man's land in cardboard boxes or wrapped in newspapers, and how the people who had to cross the Zone to get home were scared of them.

20. Scene revealing how I masturbated in my bed or in the hot house in the courtyard, and how once my mother caught me doing it, and told me that if I continued to do that I would become blind.

21. Scene describing how at the beginning of the war, before the Germans arrived in Paris, during a bombardment alert, my father and I stood at the open window of our apartment to watch the German planes bombard the Renault factory in Malakoff. It was like the fireworks on Bastille day. My mother, before going down to the shelter with my sisters, and the other people in the building, shouted at my father to go down to the shelter, but my father refused, and I was proud to stay with him during the entire alert.

22. Describe how on Sunday, my mother, my sisters, and I would walk from Montrouge all the way to Rue Vercingétorix in the 14th arrondissement, to have lunch at my grandmother's with the aunts, uncles, and cousins, and how my sisters and I always complained that it was too far to go, and that we should take the subway or the autobus, because our feet hurt, and how my mother would tell us we could not afford the metro or the autobus, and how my father never came with us on Sunday because everybody in my mother's side of the family hated him.

23. Tell how when we walked home to Montrouge after the visit to my grandmother's, we always went before it was dark because we were afraid of the *Sidis* in the Zone.

24. Tell how, when I was old enough to take the subway alone to go visit my aunts on my father's side and play with their children who lived in the Jewish neighborhood of Le Marais, I would make a detour to Rue St. Denis to look at the prostitutes standing in the street.

25. Tell how I always dreamt of becoming a great adventurer. An explorer. Or else a stowaway on a pirate ship. I also dreamt of being able to fly.

26. Tell how once my mother bought me un éclair au chocolat for my birthday.

27. Tell how I liked to go to the open market with my mother to do the food shopping.

28. Describe how the man who delivered the coal for the building where we lived dropped it from his truck in the street, and how my uncle Leon would make me carry it to the cellar with a big pail.

29. Describe how I would sneak into the Montrouge cinema, Place de la République, to see the Charlie Chaplin movies.

30. Describe how Yvette, the pretty young woman who lived on the same floor we did, one day asked me, when I was only eight years old, to come to her place to show me how to make myself feel good.

31. Tell about the stolen spoon.

32. Describe how my father used to take me with him to Place de la Bastille to demonstrate with the Communists against the government, and how we all sang the International, and how one day the police dispersed us by striking us with their sticks, and how my father got hit on the head and was bleeding, and how he wiped the blood with my handkerchief, and how my mother screamed when she saw the blood on my handkerchief, and how she told my father that he should never take me again, that he was trying to have me killed, and how I loved those demonstrations.

33. Describe how one day my father packed his little Polish suitcase and said he was going to Spain to fight with the republicans against Franco, and when my mother started crying and screaming my father screamed even louder than her, and how we the children were so scared because they were screaming so loud, we hid in the kitchen, and how when my aunt Marie heard the screaming she came up to our apartment to see what was going on, and when my mother

explained while still sobbing that my father wanted to go to Spain to fight against Franco, my aunt Marie started screaming at my father that he was a *salopard,* that he had no right to abandon his wife and children, that he was a stupid Communist, and that he would die before reaching Spain because of his tuberculosis, and how my father threw his little Polish suitcase against the wall and walked out of our apartment slamming the door and cursing aunt Marie, and we even heard him arguing with my uncle Leon in the staircase, and how my father finally came home three days later, and nobody ever talked about that scene again.

Well, good enough. I'll stop this list here. I'm sure there'll be other scenes to describe. But perhaps I've already said enough about some of these, I won't have to say more.

Federman, that would be a good place for you to tell the story of the savings account booklet.

Yes, why not, even though the funny part happened after my childhood.

At the end of each school year prizes were distributed. I don't recall how old I was, but one year I won the first prize. I don't know if it was because of the good work I had done or if it was just for my good behavior. In class, I always conducted myself well. I didn't talk with the other boys, I listened to the teacher attentively when she gave us dictations. I always turned my homework in on time. And above all I learned by heart all the poems we had to recite in class. I loved poetry.

I still remember some of these poems I had to memorize in school. Sometimes I recite to myself these crumbs of poetry.

There was one poem that I particularly liked, and that I still recite sometimes. Well, the few lines that I remember. It's a poem by Victor Hugo called "Oceano Nox."

I liked the title even though I didn't know what it meant before the teacher explained it to the class.

Here are some of the lines I remember. I quote them in French since I memorized them in French.

Oh! Combien de marins, combien capitaines
Qui sont partis joyeux pour des courses lointaines,
Dans ce morne horizon se sont évanouis!
Combien ont disparu, dure et triste fortune!
Dans une mer sans fond, par une nuit sans lune,
Sous l'aveugle océan à jamais enfouis!

I suppose I should attempt to translate that for those readers who may not know French. But I won't bother with the rhymes.

Oh, how many sailors, how many captains
Who left joyfully for far away places
Have vanished beyond the bleak horizon!
How many have disappeared, hard and sad destiny,
In a bottomless sea, during a moonless night
Buried forever under the blind ocean

That's the best I can do for now. Ah, Victor Hugo, *hélas!*

I have forgotten the rest of the poem, except for two more lines.

On s'entretient de vous parfois dans les veillées,
Tandis que vous dormez dans les goémons verts!

I loved that word *goémons*, even though I never knew what a *goémon*
was. In fact, I had to look it up in my French-English dictionary in order
to be able to translate it.

Sometimes during evening gatherings we speak of you
While you are asleep amongst the green seaweed.

That's good enough.

Back then, as a boy, I wanted to be a sailor who would sail joyfully to far
away places. A deck-boy on a big ship. Perhaps even on a pirate ship.

To fall asleep amidst the green seaweeds.

Here I am, again entangled in a dreamy digression.

I was saying in school I always did my work well. Perhaps I was not as dumb as I was made to believe, even if my uncle Leon and my cousin Salomon always called me *petit con* because I never had much to say.

Often at the end of the school week I would come home with *bons points*. In my school you would get *bons points* for good behavior. They looked like little stickers.

They had no value, except that they made my mother happy when I brought them home. And me, I was proud to get these *bons points*. I kept them in a small box.

As I said, it was probably more for good behavior than for my good grades that I was awarded the first prize that year. Good behavior in my school counted more than good work.

In any case, the day of *la remise des prix* my mother was very proud of me. She came to the ceremony with my two sisters. My father was not there.

When one of the teachers called my name I had to get my prize from the principal. I was very nervous and all flushed. The principal was seated behind a table on the stage of the auditorium with all the prizes in front of him. Seated next to him there was a man from *La Caisse d'Éparge de Montrouge*. He was wearing a black suit and a bow tie. In front of him, on the table, there was a big green register in which he asked me to sign my name.

I carefully signed, making beautiful curls to the R of Raymond and the

F of Federman, the way I had learned to do in class when we wrote compositions. And I was very careful not to make ink spots while writing my name because I was so nervous. In those days we still wrote with a *porteplume* that we dipped into an ink well.

After that the principal shook my hand and congratulated me as he handed me a savings account booklet and a beautiful book bound in leather with the title on the cover inscribed in gold letters. It was *Les lettrres de mon moulin* by Alphonse Daudet.

The parents who had come to the ceremony applauded. I was really proud when I went back to sit next to my mother who kissed me on the cheek. She was so proud of me, even though the other boys were looking at me enviously.

In this savings account booklet there was the sum of one hundred francs. Old francs of that period. The man from the bank explained when he handed me the booklet that I was the only one authorized to collect this money, but not before I became *majeur*. That is to say before I was twenty-one years old.

My mother put that booklet in the cardboard box with the family papers and photos she kept in the little closet next to her bed. And that's where I found it after the war when I returned to Montrouge from the farm.

I took these old papers and photos with me when I left for America, and also the savings account booklet thinking that it would be a nice souvenir from my school days in Montrouge.

It didn't occur to me then, in 1947, to try and collect that money.

Eleven years later, when I returned to France for the first time, thinking that perhaps I would remain there, and never go back to America, I took all the old papers and photos with me, as well as the savings account booklet.

I had not done very well in America. I was almost thirty years old and still a student. I wanted to finish my studies, but especially the novel I had started writing. A novel that has remained unfinished and which will never be published. *Une oeuvre de jeunessse*, even if I was no longer a young man when I was writing it. The book was called *And I Followed my Shadow*. I wrote it in English. I was relating in a sentimental and disorganized fashion what had happened to me during the

war. But to tell the truth, I had no idea as to how one writes a novel. Still, I wanted to finish it, and I thought that if I returned to France I could perhaps recall better what had happened.

So, before leaving Los Angeles where I was studying at UCLA, I sold all my things, my bicycle, most of my books, my jazz records, even some of my clothes, and I bought a plane ticket.
With my knowledge of the English language I was sure that I would be able to get some kind of job in Paris where I would finish my novel.

Well, no need to go on with what happened, and why I went back to Los Angeles after a few months. That return to France was a total disaster. I told all that in **Aunt Rachel's Fur.**

But I must tell you the story of the saving's account. I am in Paris for three weeks already, but no job. Nothing. No one wants to hire me. I am told that knowledge of English does not suffice. One must have experience. And me, I had no experience, except as a factory worker, or a waiter, or a dishwasher, and a dozen other pitiful jobs which I had done before being called into the army and sent to Korea to fight the war for America. So here I am, totally broke, and not the right kind of experience.

It was then that I remembered that savings account booklet. Why not try to collect the money, I told myself. After more than twenty years these hundred old francs must have accumulated some interest. And besides, now I am *majeur*.

So I go to the Montrouge Savings Bank. I show the booklet to the lady at the information desk. She looks puzzled. Finally she says to me, Well, you know Sir, this booklet dates back to before the war. I don't think it's still valid. In any case, all the archives of those years are now in the main office of the Paris Savings Bank, Rue Vaugirard in the Quinzième Arrondissement. Perhaps if you go there, they might be able to help you.

So, I said to myself, why not try? What do I have to lose?

Here I am at the main office of the Paris Savings Bank. I show my booklet to the lady at the information desk. The same puzzled look.

After examining the booklet from all sides, she tells me with a motion of the head that seems to indicate that there isn't much hope for me to collect this money, that I must go up to the archives on the third floor, and that perhaps there I can find out if I can be payed.

I am now on the third floor in a large somber and dusty hall. An older man wearing a grey tablier, with a pencil over his ear, and a number of other pencils sticking out of the chest pocket of his long jacket-like-apron, greets me. He looks like the typical *rond-de-cuir*. The perfect bureaucrat. After I explain why I am here, he examines the booklet suspiciously. He shrugs his shoulders as if to say, What can I do?

Finally he asks, How old were you when you received this booklet?

Oh, I cannot really remember, I reply. Isn't there a date in the booklet?

Once again he examines the booklet. And with his finger he shows me a date. 1937.

1937! Then I must have been eight years old. Yes, that's how old I was.

He tells me to wait and disappears at the end of the hall. A few minutes later he comes back with a huge green dusty register.
I seem to recognize the register as the one into which I inscribed my name the day of the award of the school prizes.

He places it on a table, opens it slowly, and starts turning the yellowed pages. He licks his finger each time he turns a page. He does it very carefully as if afraid that the pages will disintegrate.

The names on the pages are in alphabetical order. He pronounces the first letter of each name as he turns the pages. He arrives at the letter F. And with his finger he follows on the page the names that begin with the letter F.

Féderman, he asks, with one N or two? The way he pronounces my name, he makes it sound at if there is an accent over the first E.

One N only, I tell him. And no accent.

Ah, there it is! His finger has stopped on my name. I lean over his shoulder to look where his finger is pointing. Yes, that's my name. Raymond Federman. That's the signature I made more than twenty years ago. The one with the beautiful curls.

Yes, that's my signature, I tell him. I remember when I did it. It was during *la distribution des prix à l'école de Montrouge*. But the old man doesn't seem to be listening to me.

May I see your *carte d'identité,* to verify your signature and make sure you are Raymond Federman, the old man says with a certain authority in his voice.

When I returned to France in 1958, I didn't have a French identity card. I had an American passport. I was an American citizen.

I told in **Smiles on Washington Square** how I became an American citizen in Tokyo during the Korean war. So I'm not going to repeat that story, though it was a very funny event.

When the old man sees my American passport he looks at me like some kind of eccentric. For a moment he stands there totally baffled. Then he tells me to wait here and he goes out of the hall of archives with the green register under his arm and my passport in his hand.

This time I wait for quite a while. I am starting to find the situation amusing.

Finally the old man returns, but this time together with half a dozen people. Curious employees of the bank who wanted to see this American who came to claim money from the Savings Bank.

The old man explains that we must go to the office of the director of the bank on the sixth floor. So here we are all going up the grand staircase of this institution. The old man leading the way, me following behind, and behind me a long file of bank employees. The rumor had now circulated throughout the entire building that an American was here claiming that the Bank owed him money. I even heard someone whisper, It's like the Marshall Plan in reverse.

We are now in the office of the director. The old man explains the matter. The director examines the register and my passport with his thick eyeglasses at the tip of his nose. He looks at me. Tells me to approach. Again he examines the register and my passport with a perplexed look.

I should mention that on that day I was properly dressed. I had put on a jacket, the only one I owned, and even a tie. So I assume I gave the impression that I was not a beggar.

You are Monsieur Raymond Federman? The director asks.

Yes. Yes, I am.

And it is you who signed this register of the Montrouge Savings Bank.

Yes, it was me. In 1937, when I was a kid ... a school boy.

Well, I suppose we have to pay you your money then since you are the same Raymond Federman who signed that register when you were a school boy.

I approve with a nod of the head, and thank him.

But, the director says, I have to ask you to sign a receipt. And he slides a sheet of paper before me on his desk and shows me where to sign.

I sign.

He examines my signature. He examines the signature in the old register. He goes back and forth between the two.

You know, he tells me, the signature you just made is not the same as the one in this book.

The old man leans over the director's desk to look at the signature I just made.

Yes, it's true, he exclaims. This is not the same signature.

I am on the verge of bursting into laughter but I hold back, and explain to the director and the old archivist and to all the curious bank employees who also leaned over the desk to examine the two signatures that twenty years had passed between these two signatures. I was just a boy when I made this one, I say, pointing to the signature in the register. It's a school boy signature. A childish signature. I am now an adult, and of course my way of signing has changed. It's normal.

The director seems to approve but says, Still, it's curious.

Yes, it's true, he finally says, signatures do change with age. He takes out a sheet of paper from the drawer of his desk and scribbles something on it, and gives it to the old archivist. This is my authorization, he says, you can take Monsieur to the cashier, I believe he has a right to collect his money.

We are now at the cashier with the curious people still mumbling around me.

The chubby lady inside the cashier's cage looks at me with a kind of angry look. She must think I am a thief. She counts each bill with a scornful look as if it were her own money she was giving me. All in all she gives me 183 francs and some small coins. My hundred pre-war francs had almost doubled.

I couldn't resist, and said to her, *Merci madame, merci beaucoup de votre générosité et celle de la France.*

Thank you madame for your generosity and that of France.

I shoved the money into my pocket, and as I left, I felt behind me the confused and peevish look of the bank employees. Once outside I burst into laughter. The people in the street looked at me as though I was crazy. An old lady even asked me if I was okay because I was laughing so loud I started coughing. I reassured her that I was fine.

After that I took the subway to Montparnasse. I had decided to go and have a good lunch at the famous brasserie *La Coupole* , where I had never dared go before. It was famous for being the restaurant where all the Parisian intellectuals and artists congregated.

I ordered a dozen oysters, a steak tartare with *frites*, an endive salad, a delicious goat cheese, and for dessert *une crème caramel*. And with that half a bottle of Saint-Emilion. The whole thing cost me more than half of what I had collected, but it was well worth it.

Especially because, seated just across from my table, there were Jean-Paul Sartre, Simone de Beauvoir and Boris Vian. Really, it's true. They were there, having lunch at *La Coupole*. I wanted to go over to talk to them. To tell them how much I admired them. Tell them that when I left for America after the war, I thought of myself as an Existentialist, and that I had only two books with me: *La nausée* by Sartre, and *J'irai cracher sur vos tombes* de Vernon Sullivan. I didn't know at the time that Vernon Sullivan was Boris Vian. That's what I would have liked to tell them. But I didn't dare.

In any case, that day, I ate well, and had a good laugh, and...

Federman, you're such a liar.

No, I'm not. It's truth. Sartre, de Beauvoir, and Vian were there. But maybe it was not that day I saw them there. During the time I spent in Paris that year, I often walked past La Coupole. I couldn't afford to go in again, but perhaps that's when I saw them. What's the difference?

OK, I go back to my childhood.

Now I want to finish telling about my father. How sometimes he didn't come home for several nights. According to what I heard my aunts saying, he was sleeping with his mistress. But my mother would tell them, it's not true. That he was working.

I told earlier about the cardboard box I found in the bedroom closet, and that there were photos in it. A photo of my sisters and me when we were little. The only photo I have of them. And a photo of my parents. Their wedding photo, I think. A few photos of my father. He liked to be photographed. One of these is of him as a young man. It shows how handsome he was.

That photo is half torn, but that's the one I like best because it has a kind of symbolic meaning for me. How my father was torn from life. There is also a photo of my maternal grandmother seated with my cousin Salomon as a baby on her lap, and standing on one side of her, my aunt Marie in a beautiful flowered dress, and on the other side my mother wearing an ugly black dress that went all the way down to her ankles. It must have been the dress she had to wear in the orphanage. I suppose that once in a while my mother was allowed to leave the orphanage to visit her family.

Did I forget to mention that my mother was raised in an orphanage?

For details about the reason why my Mother spent some ten years in an orphanage after her father died in 1910, in a flood, see pages 140-141 of **Aunt Rachel's Fur.**

Besides these photos, which I took with me to America, I found two photos of two different women I could not recognize. Both were very beautiful and elegantly dressed. They were not my aunts. As far as I can remember, I had never seen these women.

One is leaning against a curtain in a provocative pose. The other is seated at a table her legs crossed.

The photos are postcards, the kind that were fashionable at that time. I don't know why, but I kept these two photos.

On the back of the photo of the woman standing by the curtain is written: *En me regardant pensez que je pense tout le temps à vous.* And it is signed, *Léa.*

I'll translate. While looking at me, think that I think of you all the time.

On the back of the other photo of the beautiful lady sitting at the table is written: *Caresses, Pauline.*

I don't think I need to translate.

While I don't want to draw any conclusions on the basis of these two photos, they do seem to confirm what my aunts were saying about my father, that he was a womanizer.

My aunts also said that my father was a gambler. That instead of working, he spent his time at the race track, or in cafes playing cards for money.

It's true that my father was not home very often, and when he was there it was to argue with my mother, usually about money, or with the rest of the family, because besides everything else, as I have already told, my father was a fanatic of politics, and he always argued with everybody about politics. Especially with Leon.

My father was on the left, whereas Leon was on the right. Which is normal since Leon was rich. Rich people are always on the right. My father was a Trotskyist, or perhaps I should say, an anarchist, and he was always broke. That's why my poor mother had to clean houses for other people so that she could feed her children.

In our house, bread was sacred. If by accident my sisters or I dropped a piece of bread on the floor, we had to pick it up immediately and kiss it. It's Maman who taught us that. Also, if we put a loaf of bread on the table upside down, we had to turn it over immediately, because Maman told to us that's it brings bad luck.

When my sisters and I were still very young there was a big economic crisis in France, and because we were poor our mother would take us to the soup kitchen. She was so ashamed to have to take us there. My sisters and I didn't mind. We even had fun standing in line with the other poor people of the neighborhood.

I wrote this poem describing how we stood in line at *la soupe populaire*, and how ...

OK, go ahead Federman, stick another one of your old poems here. If your publisher doesn't like it, he can always take it out before publishing the book.

Personally, I believe that my poems, especially those about my mother and father add a personal and emotional dimension to what I am writing about my childhood.

So, I'm not going to ask permission, I'll put my poems where I think they should be.

The Soup Kitchen

when we stood in line
at the soup kitchen
while our father
was losing our food
at the race track
betting on the wrong horse
my mother would pull the collar
of her coat up around her face
to hide her shame
but we the children
my sisters and I
we thought it was fun
to stand in line
at the soup kitchen
we would play games
counting the number of people
before us and behind us
also because we were growing children
we would always get a little extra food
and even our mother would give us
the food from her metal container
saying that she was not hungry

You know, Federman, with all this back and forth, and these poems, and digressions, and detours, your publisher is going to tell you to go take a walk. You can't just shove anything you want anywhere in your story. Your publisher is going to object.

Mister Federman, that's not what we expected from you, he will tell you. How can our readers follow what you are writing if in the middle of a story you start another story without finishing the one you were telling? We were hoping for something more readable, more accessible from you. Something less incoherent. Less surfictional. And also all those references to your other books will certainly affect the sale of this one.

Yes, I know that I never manage to get to the end of what I am telling, but that's because now that I have, so to speak, fallen back into childhood, everything gets crowded in my head.

When children tell a story they say anything that comes to their minds in any old way, and in so doing, they poeticize without realizing it.

Well, that's how I want to tell my childhood. In a kind of poetic disorder. After all, my childhood was pure chaos, incoherence, and incomprehension. And on top of that starvation. Or what the French call, crève la faim.

Ah, crève la faim! *How many times during my childhood did I tell my mother, Maman I'm still hungry. And my mother would say, Tell that to your father, while sliding from her plate into mine the rest of her food.*

Tell that to your father, she would say. My father who was losing the grocery money at the race track in Auteuil or at the Café Métropole, Porte d'Orléans, where he spent most of his time playing cards with his friends. All of them foreigners, Communists. I know because often my mother would send me to the Café Métropole to tell my father to come home.

Federman, stop! Stop! We just wanted to warn you that the way you're telling this story may not be what your publisher is expecting. And here you go jumping into another story about your father and his gambling.

This is not the place for that. These pages, these special pages in italics are reserved for comments and reflections about the way you're telling your childhood.

Then in this case, I'll go back to the regular pages, the pages of the stories, and I'll go on with what I was saying.

I really never knew my father. He was a stranger, even at home. How then can I describe this stranger who accepted to live with us? How to recognize him? That inexplicable man absent from the world. How to thank him for having given me his name to contemplate, to preserve, to surpass?

It's possible that the marriage of my father to my mother was arranged. As I said my mother was raised in an orphanage. And I understand that when young women left the orphanage they were given a small dowry, and in some cases a husband was found for them. Well, that's what I've heard.

The orphanage was called *La Maison Rothschild*. As the name suggests, it was a Jewish orphanage. My mother once showed me where it was in *le douzième arrondissement*. I don't remember why my mother and I were in that neighborhood. We were walking past a tall wall and my mother said to me, You see, behind this wall, that's where I spent most of my childhood, until I was old enough to be on my own. Your uncle Maurice and your aunt Rachel where there too. It was then an orphanage.

In those days, it was not unusual for Jewish marriages to be arranged. It was a time when many Jews from Eastern Europe were emigrating to France, many of them illegally. My father had just arrived from Poland without any papers, probably broke, and the orphanage found a Jewish husband for my mother who was still unmarried at the age of twenty-four. He was two years younger than her.

In any case, that's my hypothesis, the reason why my mother married a man who made her so unhappy all the time.

It's true that my mother was not beautiful. But she was a saint, as her sisters always said, because she endured this bastard of a husband, and sacrificed herself for her children. True, my mother was not very good-looking. She was short. Had a prominent nose, like mine. And she was crossed-eye. She wore spectacles all the time. Her hair was messy. She never used make-up. And she was always poorly dressed. Most of her clothes came from her sisters after they were used or no longer in style. But my mother was a saint.

I will not try to justify my father's conduct. I simply say how it was. Papa for me has become a mythical being. At least, that's how I imagine him. How I've reinvented him.

When I think of him, I see him in a cloud of cigarette smoke in the back of the Métropole café, playing cards with his foreign friends.

Often my mother would send me to the Métropole to tell Papa to come home for dinner. It was a ten minute walk each way to Porte d'Orléans. I was well known at the Métropole. My father's friends would kid me when they saw me arrive. Ah, here is *Schimele-Bubkes-Zinn* who comes to get Papa.

Schimele-Bubkes-Zinn, the little piece-of-shit-son of Simon. That's what they always called me.

My father would say, Wait till we finish this game and I'll come with you. So I would sit on a chair next to the table where he was playing and watch the game. That's how I learned to play *belote*, and I too became a gambler. I think in English this game is called klaberjass, or something like that.

I must tell how, in the afternoon, after I finished my homework, and managed to slip past Leon's atelier to play in the street, my school friend Robert Laurent and I would sit on the edge of the sidewalk and play *belote*. We did that almost every day. Sometimes he would win, and other times it was my turn.

I don't know why, but I have never forgotten Robert Laurent's name. Not so with the names of the other boys in school. They have all been forgotten. But not his name.

Oh, I know now why I haven't forgotten Robert Laurent's name. Or rather Bébert's as everyone called him.

Bébert was timid like me, so he didn't have many friends. That's why we played together.

My uncle Leon used to say that Bébert's parents were anti-Semites, and that I shouldn't play with him.

But we got along well, Bébert and me. Not only did we play cards together, but we also went swimming together. We were both members of a swimming club called *L'Amicale de Natation*. Every Thursday we would go practice with the team in the municipal swimming pool, rue Saillard near Denfert Rochereau. We had races against other clubs, and I even won some medals. I specialized in the backstroke, and Bébert in the butterfly. We also swam relays together.

I became a pretty good swimmer when I was a boy. Later, when I went to America I swam for Northern High School in Detroit, and then for Wayne University. In 1948, I almost qualified for the Olympic team. I'm not kidding. For more details about that see ***Take It or Leave It.***

I should tell how Bébert and I became members of *L'Amicale de Natation*. It's a funny story. We were still very young when we began swimming. We were hardly ...

And here goes Federman, launching once again into another detour.

I can't prevent myself. A word, a name from my childhood comes to me, like the name Bébert, and paff, here I go! Another story gets going.

So are you going to tell us how you became a swimmer now, or you are going to postpone that for later?

Alright, I'll tell about swimming now. But first I still have to tell why I have never forgotten the name Robert Laurent.

It's because the day I went to school for the first time with the yellow star on my clothes, that day, when I asked Bébert if we were going to play *belote* after school, he said, No, my parents told me I can't play with you any more, I can't talk to you any more.

That's what Robert Laurent said to me in 1942. It was as if I had suddenly become a pariah because of the yellow star on my chest. As if I had a contagious disease.

I suppose, that's a good enough reason for not having forgotten his name. But there is a better one also.

When I returned to France for the first time, after having spent some ten years in America, one day, by chance, I stumble on Bébert. It was in a Montparnasse café. I was sitting there alone. I see Bébert enter the café and I recognize him immediately. And he recognizes me. We were both almost thirty years old now, but still looking the same. Without my inviting him, he comes over to my table and sits down. Even offers to buy me a drink. So we talk. Or rather he talks. He tells me he knows what happened to my family during the war, and he's really sorry. He tells me how he became champion of France in the butterfly when he was twenty years old. But now he no longer swims. He tells me he still lives with his parents in Montrouge, in the same building, and that he works in a factory where they make tubes for toothpaste. It's a boring job, but he makes a decent living. He would like to get married, but has not yet found the right *gonzesse,* the right broad.

I smile when he says *gonzesse.* A good slang word I oftren used when I was living in France.

He goes on and on. I listen. I don't say much about myself when he asks what I'm doing. Except to tell him that I now live in America. And that I am a writer. What else could I tell him.

He doesn't seem interested in what I have become.

At that time, even though I had lived a rather chaotic life since the day I came out of the closet, done many crazy things, I hadn't accomplished much. For three years I worked on a farm in southern France before leaving for America. And there I worked in Detroit, and I was jazz musician, a dishwasher in New York, a waiter in a country club in the Catskills, I jumped out of airplanes with the 82nd Airborne Division in North Carolina, fought the war in Korea, did a lot of screwing with cute Japanese girls in Tokyo, went to Columbia on the G.I. Bill, and yet in spite of all that there was little to tell. Now I was just a graduate student at UCLA working on a Ph.D. Doing a lot of reading. *Le nouveau roman*. Beckett. Writing a little. Mostly poetry. I started a novel which was not going very well. I hadn't published anything. At thirty, I felt like a failure.

I didn't tell Bébert all that. I was only thinking about it while he went on telling me about his mediocre life. I let him talk. I was impatient for him to leave.

Finally as he stood up to leave, he said to me, Why don't you come for dinner one evening, in spite of it all.

He said it in French of course. *Viens quande même dîner chez nous un soir.*

I don't know why, but I said, Yes, that would be nice. It was, I suppose, his *quand même* that made me accept his invitation. Let's say that I was curious to see how anti-Semites lived now.

And besides that it'll give me a chance to see the old neighborhood.

Come this weekend, he said, as he waved *au revoir*.

So the following Saturday, I arrive at Bébert's parents. Same old building, on my street, rue Louis Rolland. I'm greeted warmly. As if I were an old friend of the family. Bébert's mother even kisses me on both cheeks. His father shakes my hand vigorously. Before sitting at the table for dinner we talk. I am asked what kind of work I do, what kind of writing, how it is to live in America, if I'm doing ok over there. Just banal conversation. We avoid talking about what happened during the war. I am wondering why I decided to come.

Bébert's mother goes back and forth between the dining room and the kitchen where she's preparing dinner, finally she brings out a big soupière, puts it on the table and says, Dinner is served, let's eat before the soup gets cold.

I am sitting next to Bébert facing his mother. She tells me to serve myself. I fill my plate with what looks and smells delicious. I love split pea soup, I tell Bébert's mother. As I reach for my soup spoon, I notice the initials carved on the handle. It's a silver spoon. I look at it.

M.F. These are the initials on that spoon. And suddenly I realize that I am holding in my hand a silver spoon that belonged to my mother. Yes, my mother had a set of silverware with her initials. I believe it was a gift from her sisters when she got married. We never used that silverware. It stayed in a drawer of the buffet wrapped in newspaper. Whenever my mother complained to my father that she didn't have enough money to buy food, my father would threaten to take the silverware to a pawn shop.

My mother would stand in front of the buffet to protect her silverware, and start crying. So my father would not insist. I think he respected my mother's personal treasure.

I remained seated at the table for a moment, my hand holding the spoon before my face, my eyes fixed on it. Then I put it down slowly on the table. Got up. I didn't say anything. They all had lowered their heads over their soup. I stood by the door a moment, looking at them, and then I left. I felt a heavy silence behind the door.
I was not going to ask them to give me back the spoon, and whatever else they had stolen from us. I can still see Madame Laurent's face when I held the spoon before my eyes staring at the initials. She looked as if she was ready to burst into tears or choke with sobs. She was all flushed. Monsieur Laurent just kept his head down, he started eating his soup. Bébert attempted to rise from his chair as if he wanted to reach for me, but he froze there.

Well, enough of that. But I believe that is the real reason why I have never forgotten the name Robert Laurent. And why I ...

As I was finishing writing the scene about the spoon the phone rang. My daughter from New York long distance, or wherever she is right now. She's always on the move.

She asks what I am doing.

Writing, I tell her. I just finished a new scene for the novel Shhh. *You want me to read it to you?*

I often read what I'm writing to Simone when she calls. This way I get feedback. She's tough. She knows how to tell me when I go overboard, as she's fond of saying. That doesn't mean she's always right, but I listen to her.

Is it funny? she asks.

Not really. Well, you'll see.

So I read her the scene about the spoon.

Pop, you're not going to stick that in the novel. It's not true. I never heard this story before. You've invented the whole thing to be more dramatic. To have people feel sorry for you. You fabricated that spoon story. Besides it's not plausible. Especially since you say all the time that your parents were very poor. How come then your mother had all that silver?

It was a wedding present from her sisters.

I don't believe that. When your mother got married her sisters must have been just as poor as she was. They couldn't afford to buy her such an expensive gift. Maybe later they got rich. And besides those aunts of yours all seem rather stingy.

Pop, the whole scene is too melodramatic. Doesn't sound real. Especially the chance encounter with Bébert in a café. It's not believable. I doubt you would have recognized each other. And even if you did, I doubt he would have invited you for dinner. If I were you I would take that scene out of the book immediately. The fact that you remember the name of the guy, that's good enough. No need to explain why you remember it. Explanations always falsify the truth.

She's something, my daughter Simone, the theater director, especially when she gets carried away like that. She's always right, even when she's wrong.

109

I should have told her that readers of fiction like to be told sad stories, as long as they appear to be true. I mean convincing, and the chronology is faithful to the principle of non-contradiction. It is well known that testimonies cause indignation and make those who listen feel good. What I wrote in that scene is a kind of testimony of what happened at that time, not only to us, but to many Jews who were deported. Their things, their possessions were stolen. Especially the silver and the works of art.

That's what I wanted to explain to Simone after her ranting about what I had written. But she hung up too soon. She had to rush somewhere.

Anyway, I'll tell how Bébert and I became members of L'Amicale de Natation.

Before the day when Bébert told me he couldn't play with me any more, we were good buddies. It's with him that I smoked my first cigarette. Sometimes Bébert and I stole cigarettes from our father's packs. We did all kinds of things like that, Bébert and me. We would steal candies from the candy store, but I'm not going to tell how we did it because all children steal candy from candy stores too. But I'll have to tell later how I stole a ring from a department store and how I got caught.

I'll have to tell that. I'm not sure if I've mentioned it in the list of scenes to relate. But I'll make a note to myself now not to forget.

I'll go on with Bébert and *la natation*.

One day Bébert tells me that he had gone to a swimming pool for the first time. We were still very young when he told me that. And he said that I should come with him next time. It's a lot of fun, you'll see. And this way we'll learn how to swim.

When I told my mother that I wanted to go to the swimming pool with Bébert, she told me that I would need a bathing suit. But for the time being she couldn't afford to buy one.

I had never been in water before. I mean my whole body. Not even in a bath tub. When I was still young my mother would wash me in the kitchen in a wash basin. When I became too old and too big for the wash basin, my father would take me to the public baths of Montrouge once a week for a shower. I liked taking a shower, but it was not like being completely inside the water.

My mother would always tell me to make sure to dry my hair well so that I wouldn't catch a cold when I came out of the public baths.

I don't know how my mother managed it, but a few days after I told her I wanted to go swimming with my friend Bébert, she gave me a swimming suit.

I was the little darling, *le chouchou* of Maman, and when I wanted something somehow she always managed to get it for me. I still remember this bathing suit. It was dark blue, and it had a little red anchor on the side. I kept it for a long time even after it became too tight for me.

The day my mother gave me the bathing suit, my sisters complained that it wasn't fair, that it was always me who got extra things from Maman. They also wanted bathing suits, even if they didn't go swimming. My mother told them she would try to get them each one.

I think my sisters did get bathing suits. Yes, when the three of us went on vacation one summer with *les colonies de vacances* organized by the city of Montrouge for the children of poor families. But it was …

Federman, why don't you ever say how old you were when you tell one of these stories of your childhood. You say, I was still a small boy, I was little, or I was older and bigger, but you never give the exact age. It's confusing.

The reason I don't tell how old I was is because it's impossible for me to remember exactly. I am trying to tell thirteen years of my life. Thirteen years of confusion and obliviousness. So I cannot organize chronologically with precise references the age I was.

From time to time, I do give a date. And since you know when I was born, it's up to you to calculate.

OK, this is how I became a member of L'Amicale de Natation.

The day I got my bathing suit I went to the swimming pool with Bébert, and that day I almost drowned. This is what happened.

At the swimming pool there were cabins in which to undress. So I took off my clothes, folded them neatly, and put on my bathing suit. I was a bit ashamed to come out of the cabin because my body was so white and skinny. The boys who were swimming in the pool were all suntanned. It was summer. Timidly, I approached the edge of the pool and watched how people were swimming. It looked like it was easy to stay on the surface of the water by slapping it with your arms and legs. While I was watching, two big boys approached me and started shoving me around.

I had forgotten to take off my socks. I hadn't realized. The two boys kept laughing and pushing me and suddenly I fell into the pool. In the deep end. Since I had never been in the water before I didn't know what to do. My arms were flailing about, but I was sinking. I had water in my mouth, in my nose. I panicked. When the life-guard saw that I was drowning, he jumped in and pulled me out. He stretched me on the side of the pool, and made me breathe by pressing on my chest. I was trembling. All the boys were standing around me, some of them still laughing because I still had my socks on, which were all wet now. Finally I was able to stand up. I was so ashamed, but I didn't cry.

When Bébert saw what had happened he came to get me and explained that when you don't know how to swim you have to stay in the shallow end of the pool. I was afraid to go in, but when I saw how he was able to stand up, and the water reached only to his waist, I climbed down the ladder on the side of the pool, and slowly entered the water. I stayed close to the edge, holding on to it. It felt good to be in the water. But I didn't dare duck my head down like Bébert was doing.

After that, every Thursday Bébert and I went to the swimming pool. Little by little we both became more daring. We imitated how the other boys who could swim were moving their arms and legs, but we did it only in the shallow end and not far from the edge. After a while we were able to stay on the surface of the water without having our feet touch the bottom of the pool.

One day a man who was there every Thursday showed us how to move our arms and legs to do the breaststroke. Soon Bébert and I were able to swim across the narrow side of the pool.

The man who was teaching us was the coach of *L'Amicale de Natation*, and one day he told us that we could join his club for free and be part of the team that competed against other swimming clubs. The man explained that he went from pool to pool to recruit young swimmers. He told us that by looking at the bodies of young people he could determine if they could become good swimmers.

I wonder how he could determine that I could become a swimmer, me who was so skinny then, and undernourished, me whose knees knocked together when I walked, whose ribs were showing through my skin. And yet, I did become a good swimmer, specializing in the backstroke, and almost made the 1948 US Olympic Team, as I mentioned before.

My mother was pleased that I went swimming regularly. She kept saying that it was good for me, it made me stronger. But my uncle

Leon made fun of me. He would say that it was a waste of time.

Of course, when I had to wear the yellow star on all my clothes, I was no longer allowed to go to the municipal swimming pool. Nor to the movies. Nor to public libraries and museums. I even had to stop playing in the street with the other boys from the neighborhood. I would stay home and play alone, or reread my Jules Verne.

It was the same for my cousin Salomon and the other Jewish boy in our school. His name was Lucien Jacobson, but everybody called him Loulou.

Oh, that's another name from my school days that I remember. Lucien Jacobson. Of course, Loulou with whom ...

Loulou! Federman, is that the Loulou whose story you tell in Double or Nothing?

Yes, that's him.

*Those who want to know more about Loulou, and how we left together for America on the same ship, and how together we starved in New York, eating noodles every day because we were broke, and how we managed to survive, they can consult **Double or Nothing,** the noodle novel, as my friends call that book.*

Not much more to say about swimming, and the boys from my school.

Now I'll go back to the Café Métropole where I watched my father play cards.

When I went to get my father at the café, I knew when he was winning because while I waited for his game to be over, he would order *un citron pressé* for me. The days when he was losing I didn't get one. And when he came home he was always in a bad mood, and he would argue with my mother, and she would cry. My mother cried a lot in her short life.

The only day when my father would come home for dinner regularly was Friday. Not because it was the beginning of the Sabbath. In our home, we didn't pay attention to the Sabbath or any religious holidays. My father was an Atheist. So my sisters and I were raised without any religion. During my entire childhood I never set foot in a synagogue, and I knew nothing of Jewish customs. I was not even *Bar Mitzvad*. Though I was circumcised. That much I can prove. My cousin Salomon, he was *Bar Mitzvad*. And I remember how all the aunts and uncles brought him lots of presents.

Once in a while Maman would tell us about God and the Jewish religion, but she always spoke in a low voice. She had learned the religious customs in her orphanage, but she was afraid to talk about them because of my father.

Anyway. One of these customs is to eat carp on Friday before the Sabbath. And my father loved carp. So he always gave my mother extra money to buy a carp, and always came home for dinner on Fridays. My sisters and I, we didn't like eating carp, but Maman would say it was good for us, and so we were forced to eat it, except for the head with the eyes. We were scared of the head with its big eyes. But my father he ate everything, the whole head and the eyes. He ate it cold with aspic. Though, I remember how one evening Papa almost choked when he swallowed one of the fish-bones. My mother got scared. He was all red and coughing. But he finally managed to spit it out.

I liked Fridays because I could play with the carp before my mother cooked it. In the morning she would go to the fish market to buy a live carp which she kept alive all day in a wash basin full of water. The same one she used to bathe me in. My sisters didn't play with the carp because they were afraid. But me, when I came home from school I would quickly finish my homework to be able to play with the carp. I would put a wine bottle cork in the water and I would push it with my finger towards the carp as if it were a little boat, and the carp would swim away from the cork. While playing with the carp I would imagine far away places on the other side of the ocean. Except that I had never seen the ocean. I saw it for the first time when I left on the boat for America.

No, I'm mistaken. I had seen the sea, once. In Trouville. Now I remember.

Ah, the holes in memory.

I'll tell that now before I forget it again.

One day Papa came home all happy. We knew immediately that he had won money at the races. Before even taking off his coat, he emptied his pockets on the table. It was just before dinner. I was in the middle of setting the table. He pushed aside the plates and he dropped a pile of hundred francs bills on the table. A huge pile. I had never seen so much money.

My mother didn't say anything, but I could see that she was happy too because now she could buy more food, and maybe even some new clothes. But after Papa gave her some of the bills, he put the rest of the money back in his pocket, and started laughing. He picked up my little sister Jacqueline and did a pirouette holding her above his head. We were all so happy that day. And then he said, Tomorrow is Sunday, tomorrow we are all going to the beach in Trouville.

My sisters and I were jumping with joy. But my mother didn't seem very pleased about this idea of going to Trouville. She knew why Papa wanted to go there. My sisters and I, we didn't know. We didn't know that there was a casino in Trouville.

So early the next morning we took the train to Trouville. It was the first time on a train for my sisters and I.

Later, when we were a little older, we took the train twice to go on vacation. As I mentioned before, the city of Montrouge would send the children of the poor to spend two weeks on farms in Le Poitou. I'll tell more about that later. But that day, when we went to Trouville, it was our first time on a train.

We had our faces pressed against the window looking in awe at the trees speeding by, the fields, the farm houses, the cows. We were laughing, and shouting, Look, *regarde les vaches*. Oh, look over there, sheep, and a horse. We were so happy, and I think that made Maman happy too. When we arrived in Trouville, Papa bought each of us, my sisters and me, a little pail and a shovel so we could play in the sand on the beach. This was before Maman bought us bathing suits, so that day we were wearing shorts.

So here we are on the beach. It was a beautiful sunny day. Maman didn't have a bathing suit. She was wearing the dress she wore every day. She sat on one of the towels she had brought along, she pulled her dress up around her thighs so her legs could get suntanned. And she put a handkerchief on her head. It was one of the few times I saw my mother smile.

My sisters and I were afraid to go in the water. We were still very young. We were afraid of the waves. So we stayed on the edge of the surf and put only our feet in, but when the waves came rushing at us we would jump back, and the water would splash us. Maman kept calling out to us, don't go in. Be careful. Come back here and play with your pails.

As soon as we arrived on the beach, Papa said he was going for a walk. Of course, he went to the casino. I didn't know then what a casino was, but when he came back later in the afternoon Maman screamed at him for having lost all the money playing roulette.

We immediately left for the train station. We didn't even stay until evening in Trouville. We went back to Montrouge on an early train. But at least, I had seen the sea ...

You know, Federman, what you are telling is not really the story of your childhood. Except for a few anecdotes about what you did or what you endured when you were a kid, it's mostly the story of your parents that you are in the process of telling. You tell more about your father and your mother than about yourself. You don't stop talking about them.

It's true that it's about them that I say the most. Finally, this book will be their story. Well, part of their story. The beginning..

You also tell a lot about your uncle Leon, your aunt Marie, and your cousin Salomon.

You're right that Leon and Marie are very present in what I am telling.

In fact, Federman, the book you are writing is really the story of a house. The house in Montrouge in which you spent your childhood with your family, but also with Leon, Marie, and Salomon.

I do tell a lot about that house, as if it were still haunting me. Perhaps that's why I am so obsessed by it. Yes, for me it is a haunted house.

Well, to go on with the house, I'll tell now how one day my uncle Leon decided to plant a tree in the courtyard.

One day Leon decided to plant a tree in front of the house in the middle of the courtyard with a flower bed around it. When Leon decided something, no one could argue with him.

Me, I was afraid that he would make me dig the hole to plant his tree. But no. My cousin Salomon was also afraid that his father would make him plant the tree. But no. Leon said that he would do it himself because he didn't trust anyone else to do it properly.

So my uncle took off his jacket and his vest, loosened his tie, rolled up the sleeves of his shirt all the way to the black garters around the top of the sleeves. Then he carried his tree, that was not that big, but still quite heavy, to the center of the yard. Exactly at the center, because Leon had measured the distance of the yard from one wall to the other. The yard was square. That's how he was able to determine where the center was. Leon was very meticulous. And then he started breaking the asphalt that covered the entire yard to make a circle in the ground with a pickaxe so he could plant his tree and his flowers.

Once he was satisfied with the circle he had made, he began to dig into the dirt with a spade. As he worked he became more and more red and sweaty.

I forgot to mention that it was a rather hot spring day.

All the people in the building were at their windows watching him. Even the anti-Semites on the main floor.

Oh, now I remember, he was wearing suspenders. I don't know why I suddenly remember those suspenders. They were mauve, like those of Adolphe in the *Rendez-vous des Cheminots* that gave Roquentin *la nausée.*

Wow! was Leon sweating. His shirt was all wet in the back. And he was groaning as he kept digging. My uncle Leon was not a very strong man. He was tall but not very muscular. He was not built for manual labor. To sew clothes with a sewing machine is not the kind of work that requires big muscles. His skin was white, and we could see the swollen veins of his arms as he kept digging the hard ground.

Finally, when the hole was deep enough he set the tree into it, closed the hole around the roots with dirt, and then he leaned on his spade to admire his work. All the people at the windows applauded, and me too.

Leon didn't say anything. But it was obvious from the way he leaned on his spade, that he was pleased with his work. But to tell the truth, Leon's tree never grew. It remained a miniature tree. It always looked like it was dying. A moribund tree. During my entire childhood the tree never grew. Even when spring came, it had only a few leaves. But to have seen Leon plant that tree has remained a memorable day for me. I saw how my uncle Leon made himself ridiculous.

Since I am telling about my uncle Leon, I should describe the atelier where he worked. The atelier had a large window, a vitrine that opened onto the street. The people who walked past would sometimes stop to watch Leon and Marie work.

Above the window, carved into the wall, there was a sign that said *Leon Tailleur.* I remember the day that sign was carved into the wall.

Leon stood in the street, facing the house, admiring that sign with satisfaction.

Even though Leon was just a tailor in a proletarian suburb, and not one of the famous tailors in the swanky neighborhoods of Paris, he was proud of the suits he made for his rich clients.

Leon and Marie spent their entire day working relentlessly in the atelier making men's suits. From early in the morning till late in the evening, they would sew, by hand and the sewing machine. They would measure and cut the fabric, press the suits with the big steam iron, day after day, even on Sundays. The atelier was like a factory, a mini-factory. Oh, the steam iron was heated with coal on a small stove in the middle of the atelier. It was very heavy.

I spent a lot of time in that atelier because when I'd finished my homework and wanted to go play in the street, I would try to sneak past the windows of the atelier, but Leon would call me, and he would find something for me to do. Picking up with a small magnet the pins and needles that had fallen between the cracks of the wooden floor, or gathering the little pieces of cloth that had fallen to the ground when Leon was cutting the fabric with his large scissors. If there was nothing for me to do in the atelier, he would have me clean the W.C. in the courtyard. Oh, did I hate doing these chores. It made me angry. The worst was when he sent me to the cellar to get coal. But I never complained. I was too shy, too ...

Federman you've said all that before, Leon the tailor, the cellar, the rats, the out-house.

I know, I know, but I'm remembering more details. Besides, as it has been said before, the persistence of the **twofold vibration** *suggests that in this old abode all is not yet quite for the best.*

While I was doing all these chores, my cousin Salomon was upstairs supposedly doing his homework or practicing his piano, but instead he was reading the coming books that he sent me to buy for him. Or else masturbating.

In the evening, after they closed the atelier, Leon and Marie would continue to work late into the night in their apartment. So that the people in the street would not see the light, and wonder why they were working so late, they would cover the windows with blankets, the way people in the cities had to do when the war started because of the alerts. I suppose it's because Leon and Marie worked so hard that they were so rich.

Well, I think that's enough about them and their atelier.

Now I should perhaps say more about the shit-house in the courtyard, and about the staircase that always smelled as though there was something rotten in it. And I should also tell about the young woman who lived on the same floor as us, in a one room apartment to the right of the landing. Her name was Yvette. I've never forgotten her. She was beautiful. Later you'll hear what happened one day with Yvette when I was a young boy, and she ...

Federman, you know you're really going too far with these postponements, and all these I'll tell later, I'll tell later. Why don't you tell the story of Yvette now?

If I get into another detour in the middle of what I'm telling, it's going to mess up everything. There won't be any continuity in the story. I just want to finish the description of the house.

So what else is new. That's all you do is mess up continuity page after page with all your detours and digressions.

Alright then, I'll tell about Yvette now.

One day, my father tired of hearing my mother complain that he didn't give her enough money to feed the children decided to do something about it. He decided that he would make money by selling things at the flea market, *le marché aux puces* of Montrouge. Somehow he managed to borrow a hand-cart, and he and my mother loaded it with all kinds of things—kitchen utensils, pots and pans, old pieces of furniture, even used clothes. I have no idea where they got all that *camelote*, as my father called it. Probably from some of the uncles and aunts who didn't need those things any more.

My sisters and I were sitting on the curb when Maman and Papa left. Maman was in front pulling the cart with a big rope tied around her shoulders. Papa was pushing from behind.

Maman told us to be good, and to watch out for the cars in the street.

Jacqueline must have been seven years old. I was nine, and Sarah eleven. We were not afraid to stay alone. We felt very grown up to be trusted in this way.

After the cart disappeared around the corner, my sisters and I played hopscotch for a while on the sidewalk, and then we went into the courtyard to play.

Leon, Marie and Salomon were not home. They had gone to see our grandmother, as they did regularly on Sundays. I think they gave her money when they went to see her, as did the other uncles and aunts who were wealthy. Because we were poor, my mother could never contribute.

All the other people who lived in the building were also gone, except for the young woman who lived upstairs, on the same floor we did.

It was a nice sunny day. May, I think. Jacqueline was playing with her doll. Sarah was sitting on the ground her back against the wall, reading *La Comtesse de Ségur*, and I was playing with my tin soldiers who were engaged in a major battle.

Yvette, yes that was her name, was at her window combing her hair. She had long reddish hair. I don't know how old she was. I was still too young to be interested in girls. But I liked her long shiny hair, and the way she sung all the time, and how she would pinch me gently whenever we passed each other in the staircase.

From our apartment we could hear her singing. We shared the same wall. Everybody in the building liked her, except my uncle Leon who kept saying that she was a *courveh*. Papa, to the contrary, said that she was a professional singer because she had such a beautiful voice.

While my sisters and I were playing in the courtyard, Yvette called out, What are you kids doing? How come you're all alone?

And we answered, We're playing. Maman and Papa went to sell things at the *marché*.

Then she called out, Raymond come on up a minute, I want to show you something.

Curious to see what she wanted to show me, I left my soldiers in the courtyard, and went up to her apartment. The door was ajar and she was sitting on the edge of the bed. She was wearing a dressing-gown. It was lilac. At least, that's the color

I remember every time I think of Yvette. Oh, and also, the dressing-gown was slightly transparent.

I was standing at the door. Unsure about going in. Yvette said, Close the door, sweetie, and come here. So I went to her and when I was very close, standing in front of her, she began to unbutton my shorts. French boys always wore short pants in those days.

Shorts didn't have zippers, only buttons.

When she started unbuttoning me, I was surprised, but then I thought that the reason she wanted me to take off my shorts was because she was going to fix the hole I had made in the seat sliding on my behind on the ground from one side of the battlefield to the other. My soldiers were divided into two armies. The black army and the red army. And I had them spread out on the ground. The red army won most of the time because it had three soldiers on horseback. The black army didn't have any horses.

My father always said that Yvette was a nice and beautiful young lady. And if she was not a singer then she must be a model.
So that's what I thought while she was unbuttoning me. That it was very nice of her.

After my shorts were off, I stood there in my underwear, blushing, and holding my legs tightly together. I didn't know what to do. I was so intimidated. Yvette laughed gently. Then she said, Don't be afraid, take off your underpants, and your shirt too, and come and sit next to me.

Come on, little darling, don't be ashamed, take it off, she insisted. So I took my underwear off and I sat next to her all naked. Even though it was a hot day, I was trembling a little. But when she giggled, I started giggling too.

Slowly her hand touched my penis. It was not very big at that age. I had no pubic hair.

Yvette kept saying in a soft gentle voice, Don't be afraid, you'll see how good it is. She held my little thing with two fingers and rubbed it gently against my thigh. Yes, my thigh. Not hers.

Then she asked, Do you ever do that?

I shook my head and said, No, never.

You never touch it? You never hold your little *pine* in your hand? She asked, while rubbing it faster on my thigh.

Yes, I hold it when I go *pipi*.

She laughed. It's good, isn't it?

Yes, it was good. It made me feel good all over my body. I felt happy sitting there next to her while she continued to rub my cock, as she had called it, against my thigh. Then she stopped, stood up, gave me a little pat and a little kiss on the cheek, and said, Get dressed quickly now, go back downstairs to play, and don't tell anyone.

So I put my dirty underwear, my torn shorts and shirt back on, and went down into the courtyard.

My sister Sarah asked, What did she want to show you?

Oh, nothing, I replied. Just a photo of her when she was little.

My sister Jacqueline asked, Why did she want to show that photo to you and not to us?

I don't know, just like that.

Did she show you anything else? Sarah asked

Nothing, I said. And I went back to the battle of my tin soldiers. That day, the red army won again. All the soldiers of the black army were decimated, and I laughed when they all fell to the ground and died.

Yvette was back at the window, combing her hair.

After that day, often in my bed at night, I made myself feel good the way Yvette had shown me. But it took some time before I ejaculated for the first time.

I don't remember when that happened, but I got really scared in the morning when I noticed the yellowish stains in the sheet of my bed. Maman will see this. What will she say? How will I explain it?

Maman must have noticed what I had done, but she didn't say anything. She put the sheet into a big kettle of boiling water, and then she hung the sheet on a rope in the courtyard to make it dry in the sun. Later, when Maman was not looking, I went to see if my circles were still there.

After that first ejaculation, I would masturbate almost every night. But before going to bed I would sneak a piece of newspaper under the blanket to ejaculate in it. In the morning, when I was taking the dirty pail downstairs, I would toss the newspaper into it.

Speaking of newspapers, in the cabinet in the courtyard, there was no toilet paper. I mean the regular kind. We would wipe ourselves with pieces of newspaper.

Leon, was so cheap, he would cut the newspaper into little squares for us to use in the toilet, rather than buying regular toilet paper. Everybody in the building had to use this toilet, since it was the only one. Except, of course, Leon, Marie, and Salomon because, as I already mentioned, they had a toilet installed in their apartment. I used their toilet only once, when I was in their apartment and I suddenly had to go. My aunt Marie said, Go quick use the toilet, but make sure you flush it afterwards, and wipe yourself.

Sometimes when I had to go to the toilet in the courtyard, and there were no more newspaper sheets, I was forced to wipe myself with my finger which I rubbed against the wall when I was finished. I wasn't the only one to do that. There were always traces of caca on the walls of the W.C.

Whenever Leon saw that, he would make me wash the walls with a scrub brush.

Sometimes when I couldn't hold back, I would masturbate in the toilet. There was a little hook to lock the door. If I was not careful when I ejaculated the sperm would splash all over the walls, and I had to wipe it with a piece of newspaper. Afterwards, I would come out of the toilet and would feel ashamed and guilty.

My mother caught me once. She didn't get angry, but she said, If you do that again I'll tell Papa, and if you continue, you'll go blind and you'll have pimples all over your face.

I got scared when Maman told me that, so I held back for a while.

During the night when I masturbated, I would see Yvette inside my closed eyes. Yvette in her lilac negligee. I had never seen a grown woman totally naked. But because we lived in a very small apartment, sometimes I would see parts of my sisters' bodies when they were getting dressed, or when they were washing themselves in the sink in the kitchen.

Oh, this reminds me of the night when my sister Sarah had her first period. She started crying in fear not knowing why she was bleeding. Maman took her behind the curtain and calmed her down.

Maman never explained anything to us about these things. I forget how old I was when I stopped believing that children came out of cabbages, and also ...

Federman, you should be ashamed. You better stop because for sure your publisher is going to tell you that these kinds of filthy stories no longer sell in the world in which we live.

The other day I was reading the autobiography of a writer who won the Nobel Prize a couple of years ago. He was telling about his youth, but not once did he say, I masturbated, or I was jerking off, or I was giving myself pleasure alone. Not a word about that. He didn't even use the word onanism. Total silence about that. It was as though he was censuring his own life in his writing.

If I were to tell the story of my childhood without talking about the pleasure I gave myself, the story would be incomplete. It would be false.

So I'll go on with the little dirty things boys do.

In school the boys my age would tell each other how they masturbated. They would let me listen, but I never told them how I did it. There was one boy who told us how he always did it in front of the mirror because he liked to watch the grimaces he made while going full blast. Another said he loved to come in his pillow, and another while looking at photos of naked women he'd found in one of his father's books. All the other boys kept asking him to bring the book to school, but he refused. There was one boy who told the best stories. He would explain how he did it each time in a different position. Sometimes standing, or sitting, flat on his back his legs up on a chair, on all fours, on his knees. He would also demonstrate the many ways he used his hands. Sometime doing it with only two fingers, or with both hands. He had a great imagination. I envied him. But during the entire time we were in this school together I never spoke to him. Never played with him. He intimidated me. He was blond.

I was too shy to tell how I did it under the blankets or in the toilet. So the other boys would make fun of me, and kept saying, *Le fils de tubard* he doesn't know how to jerk off, he's ashamed to do it.

Ah, the dirty little things that went on in school. But I suppose it's like that in all boys' schools.

We had two *maîtresses d'école*. One was old and ugly. Always poorly dressed. She had gray hair pulled tight into a chignon. She wore black cotton stockings that were always falling down. She would not hesitate to slap us across the face if we did something wrong. She taught math and science classes. Geometry, calculus, chemistry. And also human anatomy.

The other teacher was young and beautiful, and she dressed well. She wore short skirts and silk stockings with a seam in the back, and high heeled shoes. All the boys were in love with her, even me. She liked to recite poetry to us, and made us learn poems by heart. I loved her voice.

In class she sat behind a table so that we could see her legs below the table. It was unbelievable the numbers of pencils, erasers, rulers, fountain pens that fell to the ground.

From underneath our desk we could look between her legs. We could see her white thighs above her garters. That was enough to make all of us dream of her at night. Once in a while we could even see her panties when without realizing it she opened her legs wide. The only time it was frustrating to look from under our desks was when her legs were crossed one on top of the other. Then we could see the side of her thigh, but it was not like looking between her legs.

I wonder now if she spread her legs on purpose knowing why so many pencils, erasers, rulers kept falling to the floor. Today I can speculate about that, but when I was a boy searching for my pencil under my desk, I didn't ask myself why I was doing what all the other boys were doing. I would take a quick look, and at night, under my blankets, I would try to remember what I had seen.

The funniest thing happened in her class one day. I've never forgotten it. One of the boys had taken his penis out of his pants and tied the tip with a piece of string. Then he tapped on the shoulder of the boy sitting in front of him, and handing him the end of the string he said quietly, Hold this in your hand and pull it, but not too hard.

This was happening while the teacher was reading a poem to the class. A Victor Hugo poem, I think. She was seated at her table leaning over a book, slowly reciting the poem as she scanned each syllable.

Suddenly she raised her head to see if we were listening, and that's when she saw the boy whose arm kept shaking back and forth, while holding something in his hand.

She said, Gaston ...

For the convenience of this story, I'm going to call the boy who was doing the jerking Gaston, and I'll call the other Gustave, the one whose penis was tied with the string.

... what are you holding in your hand?

Gaston blushed and said, Nothing Madame, nothing.

I can see that you have something in your hand, and that you are playing with it. Bring it here immediately.

All the boys in class started giggling because they had seen what Gaston and Gustave were doing.

So Gaston got up and walked towards the teacher still holding the string in his hand, and of course Gustave was forced to get up too and follow Gaston, holding his penis in his hand since it was still tied to the string.

When the teacher saw what Gaston had in his hand, and what Gustave had in his, she became all flushed and started screaming, You dirty little brats, I'm going to show this to the principal. And she told one of the boys sitting near the door to go fetch the principal.

Gaston and Gustave were expelled from school until after Christmas vacation. I cannot remember which year it was, but that day we all had a good laugh in that teacher's class. Perhaps even the teacher herself laughed that evening when she told that story to her friends.

I should give a name to that pretty teacher. Just to make her more *vraisemblable*. I'll call her Colette. Yes, Colette is a good name for her. As for the ugly mean teacher, I won't bother giving her a name.

Since I am telling what went on at school, I should tell what we sometimes did in the playground during recess.

Our school was like a prison. It was surrounded by a tall brick wall. There was one corner of the yard which could not be seen from the windows of the principal's office, and that's where some of the boys played ...

The Competition

Nine years old. You are in school. An all boys' school. A French school. You were born in France. It's not your fault. You had no voice in that decision.

During *récréation* some of the boys go to the far end of the yard near the big wall to play. You go with them even though they make fun of you because you're rickety and clumsy. That too is not your fault. The older boys let you play with them because they like making fun of you.

In the far corner of the yard near the big wall, where the Pion in charge of watching the boys during recess cannot see what's going on, the tallest boy draws a line on the wall above his head with a piece of chalk, while another boy draws a line on the ground about two yards from the wall. Then the boys, half a dozen of them, start the competition to see who can piss the highest above the line on the wall. You never win.

Only once did you succeed in pissing above the white line, but that's because you stood close to the wall, in front of the line, and also because you held back all the *pipi* you had in you since the night before in anticipation of the competition. You were excited to have managed for the first time to piss above the line, to piss into the sky, even if you did not win the competition that day.

The other boys said you cheated because you crossed the line on the ground. Only those who piss on the wall from the line on the ground are qualified. Those who cross the line are disqualified. That day you were disqualified as a high altitude *pisseur*.

Enough about what went on in school. Now I want to describe the game I liked to play in the street when I was alone.

On a small stick of wood, like a matchstick, I would glue a little piece of paper at one end making it look like a flag, then I would stick this flag into a cork, a bottle cork, to make it look like a small sail boat which I would put in the water that ran in the gutter, and I would follow my little boat until it disappeared into the sewer on its way to another world deep underground. A world I imagined totally different from the world I lived in. A world full of marvelous things. I was not sure what these things were, but there were always marvelous and mysterious. That was my favorite game, but I could only play it when the street cleaners let the water flow in the gutters.

When I tell someone today that I spent my impoverished childhood in Montrouge, immediately I am told, Ah, but Montrouge it's a fashionable suburb now, highly sought after by the baby boomers.

Perhaps now, but in my time Montrouge was a crummy proletarian suburb.

Though I am told that recently the Montrouge bureaucrats have given an historical name to my school. It is now called, *L'école Raymond Queneau.*

Makes me really proud to know that my school has been named after such a famous poet, especially since, without realizing it, the bureaucrats gave half of my name to the school. Normally there is no accent on Federman, but if one day the town of Montrouge decides to name a school for me, or a street—personally I would prefer a cul-de-sac—I am sure the name Féderman will have an accent. It makes it more French. As a writer who could become famous after his death, it's possible that Montrouge will name something after me, or...

Federman, now you're getting ridiculous. Who do you think you are, Victor Hugo? Finish the story, will you.

Please excuse the self-indulgent digression, and as the judge said to Maître Pathelin, revenons à nos moutons.

I was saying that during my childhood Montrouge was a working-class slum. Especially our street, because of the big smelly factory across from our house.

Mostly North Africans worked in that tannery. We called them *Sidis* because they didn't speak French like us. Everyone in our neighborhood was afraid of them. They looked mean. They all had a mustache. People said that they all carried a knife under their clothes. Some of them wore long robes. They looked like they never washed. In the evening when the *Sidis* came out of the factory, the people in the street would rush into their homes.

They lived in *La Zone*, a wasteland between Porte d'Orléans and Montrouge. This *terrain vague,* as it was called, used to surround the entire city of Paris, and that's where most of the *Sidis* lived. As I said in the list, they slept in cardboard boxes, or wrapped in newspapers. They cooked their food on small camp fires. During the winter when it was very cold, we would see them standing around their camp fires with a blanket wrapped around their shoulders. The lucky ones worked in that tannery, but many couldn't get work because they couldn't get working papers. So they had to beg.

The Zone was a dangerous place. Especially late in the evening when the people, who had gone into the city to a movie, or a restaurant on the boulevards, or a bordello, had to cross the Zone to get back to Montrouge, because the last stop of the métro was Porte d'Orléans. Sometimes they would be attacked and robbed.

From the Porte d'Orléans to Montrouge it took a good ten minutes to cross the Zone. People would walk together in groups for fear of being attacked. And if one of the beggars came close, his hand extended, saying, *Moi beaucoup faim, moi pas mangé, moi pas travail,* the people would start running. You didn't mess with the *Sidis* or else, psitt, you got a blade in your stomach.

The Zone no longer exists today. It has been cleaned out, and luxury apartments have been built there.

At the beginning of the Zone there was an *octroi,* a tax booth. All the trucks that entered Paris had to stop there to pay a toll. I don't know when all these *octrois* disappeared, but I remember them.

I also remember how during the weekend all the Parisians who had a car would drive out into the country.

My sisters and I we would sit on the curb of La Route d'Orléans and watch the cars rushing out of the city one after another in an endless parade. It was like a river of cars. This exodus would begin early on Saturday morning and continue until afternoon. A stream of cars. Small ones, big ones, old ones, new ones, limousines with chauffeurs, small trucks. Every weekend, the people who owned a car went to the countryside for picnics, or to the beach in Normandy, or to visit the castles along the Loire river, or to their country houses. And on Sunday evening they all drove back to Paris.
For my sisters and I, it was a spectacle, and so on Saturday morning we would tell Maman that we were going to watch the cars. And Maman would tell us to be careful, and to never cross the highway.

We would try to count the number of cars that rushed past, but they were going so fast we would get all confused with the numbers and had to start all over again. We never arrived at the same number.

On Sunday evening when the cars were coming back and it was starting to get dark, the headlights were like the yellow eyes of big monsters. My sisters and I were a little scared, and after a while we would hurry home.

The weekend exodus was like a ritual. All the Parisians took off to ...

Federman, since you're speaking of exodus, why don't you tell us now, as you promised in your list of scenes, how at the beginning of the war you and your parents and sisters ended up in Argentan, in Normandy, when the Germans invaded France.

Ah, yes Le Grand Exode *when the Germans were approaching Paris, and everybody took off. People were afraid of the Germans. All kinds of stories were being told about them. How mean they were. How they would cut off the hands of little boys so they wouldn't fight them when they grew up. How they would steal everything. How they would burn the cities. For me, that exodus was like an adventure. It's interesting how little has been said about that shameful moment of French history, that debacle of the French army.*

OK then, I'm going to tell the Exodus.

When the German tanks were on the verge of arriving in Paris, almost all the people in the city took off. As we did, my parents, sisters and me. And eventually we landed in Argentan.

First we went by train, and then on foot on the roads of Normandy, and finally exhausted and hungry we arrived in Argentan, that beautiful city with its splendid cathedral that later was completely destroyed by bombardments.

The great irony is that when we arrived in Argentan, the Germans were already there, waiting for us with open arms and wide smiles on their faces. They had reached Argentan before all the refugees from Paris. I remember how impressed I was by their uniforms. Especially those of the officers. These officers looked magnificent. I was dazzled by their shining black boots, their riding pants, their kepis, and the medals on their chests, but especially the revolvers in the holsters on their belts. Oh, and also the black cross tied to a ribbon they wore around their necks.

They looked like they had just stepped out of a Hollywood war movie. I felt like getting close to them to see if they were real, but my mother kept pulling me away by the sleeve.

Thousands and thousands of people not only from Paris but from other cities were on the roads of Normandy or roads that went South. Many left by trains, but when the trains reached the end of the line, they were forced to go on foot. Other people left by cars, motorcycles, bicycles. There were people pushing baby carriages and wheelchairs. They were all lugging suitcases and bags. All kinds of rumors were circulating. One was that the Germans had arrived in Paris and that the city was on fire.

We left from *Gare Montparnasse*, the closest train station from our house. We rushed through the crowded streets. People were running in all directions as if lost. There was a mad crowd at the station. People were boarding just any train without even checking where it was going. People were arguing. Pushing. It was a real panic.

When we arrived at the station we saw a bunch of people running towards a train which looked like it was about to leave. We followed them and forced our way into a car. Well, my mother forced her way in by pushing and shoving while holding on to my hand and pulling me behind her. My father behind us was holding on to the hands of Sarah and Jacqueline. It was the first time I saw my father's love for his daughters. He looked desperate. All the seats on the train were occupied. So we stood in the aisles pressed against one another. It was so crowded, when the train started rolling some people had to stand on the steps outside the doors.

The train had a steam engine. So when it accelerated the smoke drifted back into the train, people were rubbing their eyes and coughing, children were crying. People kept asking each other where this train was going, but nobody really knew. Some said that it was heading towards Normandie, but they were not sure, others that it was traveling South. But some frightened people were lamenting, Maybe it's going East where the Germans are.

I don't know how long the train had been going when suddenly it stopped in the middle of the countryside. In the middle of a forest. Someone said that the tracks were blocked with metal obstructions. Nobody knew what to do. One of the controllers who was squeezing his way between the people from one end of the train to the other, was explaining that the train could not go any further and that people should get off immediately because he didn't know what was going to happen. So people

started rushing out, pushing through the doors. Others were scrambling out through the windows. They would throw their suitcases down on the ground and jump. It was as though they had been told that the train was going to be bombarded by German planes. So people were running in all directions, disappearing into the forest. Some of them started marching along the tracks in the direction the train had been going. Others were following little paths in the forest. They were all hoping that they were going in the right direction. Away from Paris.

Many fathers were carrying little children on their shoulders, and mothers pulling them by the hand. It was hot that day, in June, 1940.

We too started walking along a path in the forest, following Papa who for once seemed to know where he was going. He had taken charge of the family. Even though it was difficult for him to breathe because of his tuberculosis. For me a great adventure had begun. I imagined the

Germans attacking us. Taking us prisoner. We were walking in a single file, my sisters and me in front of Maman who was lugging a huge suitcase full of our things. I remember, the suitcase was black, and Maman had tied a rope around it because it didn't close properly. Papa had a *musette* on his back, and his old Polish suitcase in his hand. He was walking fast, even though he kept coughing and spitting blood. Sarah, Jacqueline and I were carrying our school bags into which Maman had shoved more clothes. We walked like that a long time, twisting our ankles in the ruts of the path, until Papa was forced to stop to rest. He was coughing hard. He sat down on the ground, his head resting on his suitcase. Maman stood protecting our luggage, as other people walked past us. While Papa was resting Sarah, Jacqueline and I were gathering wild berries in the bushes along the path. They tasted so sweet, even better than the ones we sometimes got at the *marché*.

After a while we started walking again. The path led us out of the forest into an open field. In the distance we saw people walking on a road. We rushed to join them.

Once on the road we followed the others. Nobody was speaking. Even children were quiet. It was like a funeral procession. There were no houses, no farms in view, just large fields. Along the road there were cars and buses that had been abandoned because they ran out of gas. In a meadow we saw some cows. Most of them black and white. Normandy cows are usually black and white, I had learned that in school. So when saw these cows we knew we were in Normandy. West of Paris. We were sure now we were safe because we were convinced that the Germans would not go beyond Paris. That's what Hitler wanted above all, when he started the war. To conquer Paris.

Some mothers when they saw the cows went to them with cups or cans to get milk for their children. The cows stood still. They looked happy to be able to participate in this great adventure. Maybe it was me imagining they were happy. I suppose these mothers knew how to milk cows because they had been raised on farms. The milk was being passed along the line for children. My sisters and I got to drink some of that milk. It was good and warm.

A little further down the road we heard the sound of a airplane. Everybody stopped and looked up at the sky, but when the plane came over us and started shooting at us with its machine guns, people started running in all directions, diving into ditches, hiding behind trees. Some of them were wounded, others fell dead.

It was along this road in Normandy that I saw dead people for the first time. Real dead people. Not false dead people like in the movies. I was eleven. Even if I didn't understand yet what it meant to be dead, it made me feel strange to look at these people lying on the ground bleeding. Maman kept telling me not to look.

During *L'Exode*, I saw planes shooting at columns of refugees. Later I found out that these planes were not German, but Italian. They were Mussolini's planes, because Italy too was at war against France.

We kept walking. Many people had to stop along the road to rest. Those who kept going were pushing aside those who were walking too slowly. When we would hear a plane approaching, Maman would quickly push us down into the ditch alongside the road. We would cover our heads with our hands, and Maman would cover us with her body, while Papa stood tall on the road shouting Yiddish obscenities at the planes. Papa, he was scared of nothing.

It's true that this Great Exodus has been swept under the rug of French history. It was a great humiliating debacle for the French. Soldiers and refugees in retreat on the roads of Normandy.

At one point we came upon a *borne kilomérique* that said Argentan 12 kilometers. Everybody started walking faster. Twelve kilometers, people were saying, that's not far. Papa said, I don't know if I can make it. Maman told him to sit down on the ground and rest a while. She told me to take Papa's suitcase, and for Sarah to take his backpack. After a while, we started walking again. But we stopped often so that Papa could rest. He had difficulty breathing. Lots of people were passing us. Finally we arrived in Argentan.

There were German soldiers everywhere who were directing people towards Place de la République. They were very pleasant with us. They didn't push us around, didn't hit us. Some of them even spoke French. Especially the officers.

The big square was full of people. Hundreds and hundreds of them. Some were standing, others were sitting on the ground or on their suitcases. A German officer in a black leather jacket was standing on a platform speaking French with a bullhorn. I was surprised that a German spoke French so well, without an accent. Even my father who knew six languages had an accent in French.

The officer on the platform was telling us not to be afraid. That the soldiers were going to take care of us. Give us food, and find us a place to sleep.

In fact, German soldiers were already circulating in the crowd of refugees distributing bread and water. They even gave milk to the mothers with babies. We got a loaf of bread and some fruit.

Everything was so well organized. The Germans knew in advance that all these people were arriving, and they had prepared to receive them not like enemies, but like friends.

The officer on the platform then said that families with several children will be lodged first. And he told these families to step forward. So, my parents, sisters and I moved to the front. Two soldiers motioned for us to follow them.

As we walked with these two soldiers in the streets of the city, the Argentan people were watching us from their windows. They must have been wondering, who are these idiots from Paris who are so afraid of the Germans. When the Germans arrived in Argentan, a few days earlier, they were nice and pleasant with the inhabitants. They didn't demolish anything, didn't burn anything, didn't steal anything. They just took from the markets only the food they needed. And they immediately established order in the city, which was necessary since the people of Argentan became anxious and restless when they learned that German trucks were approaching. So the Germans had to put the people at ease. Especially because they panned to occupy Argentan for a long time. The only strict order which was enforced was that no one was allowed in the streets after six o'clock in the evening.

As we walked, we didn't look back at the people who were staring at us. We were ashamed to be refugees. We felt like foreigners.

Me, I was concentrating on the uniforms of the soldiers and on their rifles. I would have loved to have had tin soldiers just like them.

While we were walking with the two soldiers, Papa started talking to them in German. I don't know what he was saying, but after that the two soldiers were very nice to us. They installed us in a two-story house which was empty, except for some furniture. Then one of them went to get food for us. The one who stayed continued the conversation with my father. I was so impressed with my father. Then the soldiers left, and we settled in. For the first time I had my own room, and my sisters too. We learned later that this house had been a youth hostel, but when the war started it was closed and abandoned.

During our entire stay in Argentan, almost an entire year, these two German soldiers often visited with my father. They even brought other German soldiers along with them. They would bring their uniforms that needed fixing to my mother. A torn sleeve, a missing button to be sewn back on.

Maman became the *couturière* of these soldiers. She even washed and pressed their shirts. They were all so nice to us.

Meanwhile, once in a while, with a special pass from the *kommendantur*, Papa would take the train to Paris to buy things for the Germans. French perfume. Silk stockings. Jewelry. Chocolate. All kinds of things like that which were still available in France, but no longer in Germany since the beginning of the war. So we were comfortable in Argentan. We had a good life. A whole house for ourselves, extra money, extra food. The soldiers who became friendly with my father would always bring us food.

One of the Germans who came regularly to our house was a *Feldwebel*. A sergeant. His name was Willie Forst.

I've never forgotten that name, because my father told me that there was a famous German actor of that period who was also called Willie Forst. I don't know how my father knew that, bu tmy father knew many things.

A small group of Germans soldiers came regularly to our house in the evening to drink beer and have discussions with my father.

When they arrived, they would give me some money to go buy *des canettes de bière,* and the next day when I returned the empty bottles I would get one sou for each one.

In the evening when the Germans came to our house, my father would sit with them in one of the large rooms in the house. Sometimes he would let me stay in the room after I brought the beer. I would sit quietly on the floor in a corner of the room and listen to them talk even though I didn't understand what they were saying. After a while I would catch a few words which they often repeated. Like the word *krieg*. The words *schwer, Frau, Kinder, Arbeit*. And other words like that. I would ask Papa what these words meant, and also what they were discussing. He would tell me that they were talking about their families, about what they did before the war, things like that. But especially, my Father said, We discuss politics.

I already told in the list of scenes how before leaving all these Germans would raise their fist and sing the *International*. No need to repeat that many Communists were hiding in the German army.

We stayed a year in Argentan. This was the least unhappy period of my childhood. In the fall of 1940, I was admitted to the Lycée d'Argentan where many sons of refugees went. All of different ages. But we got along together. Except that the boys from Argentan didn't like us. When we were coming out of school they would start fights with *les parigots*, as they called us. We would throw stones at each other or chestnuts, and hit each other with our school satchels. Me too, I would get into these fights. In Argentan, I started gaining weight and getting stronger because we ate well, and I was becoming less shy.

I got my *Certificat d'étude* from the Argentan lycée with *mention très bien*. My mother and father were proud of me.

We should have stayed in Argentan. My father was doing well with the black market. My sisters and I liked the schools we were attending. In Argentan nobody cared where you came from since most of the people were refugees.

Yes, we should have stayed in Argentan, but a decree from the Vichy government announced that all the refugees had to return to their homes. So eventually we went back to Montrouge, even though Papa had arranged with the Germans for us to stay longer than other Parisians.

For me, it was as if a long vacation was ending. I hated to leave.

I wonder what would have happened if we'd stayed in Argentan. Most likely we would have been denounced as collaborators. Already the people in our neighborhood were saying bad things about us because German soldiers often came to our house.

They said it even more the day Willie Forst brought us a truck load of coal. It was the beginning of winter, and it was getting cold. The truck stopped in front of our house and unloaded the coal on the sidewalk.

After the truck left, Papa and me, and even Sarah and Jacqueline worked hard to bring the coal into the cellar of the house in buckets, while the neighbors were looking at us from their windows, and probably saying, those dirty collaborators.

I am sure that if we had stayed in Argentan, at the Liberation, people would have shaved our heads.

The irony is that my parents and sisters would have been shot in Argentan by a French firing squad as collaborators, and not as Jews in a German concentration camp.

And I would probably have been shot too. But since I am here, still alive, telling you all the things that happened during my childhood, no need to speculate.

Soon after we got back to Montrouge, my mother had to sew the yellow star on all our clothes.

Then my parents and sisters were deported to Auschwitz, and I was deported, in a manner of speaking, to the farm in Southern France where ...

Federman, maybe you should tell us what happened when you and your family were ordered to return to Montrouge. How it was living during the occupation.

Oh, it was such a sad period. Much of it has been blocked in my mind. But I'll try.

When we left the house in Argentan with our suitcases on the way to the train station, as we walked away I looked back at the house, and sadness came over me. I was twelve now, and full of apprehension about what was ahead for me.

On the train to Paris we all sat quietly. Barely talking to each other. It was as though we felt we were going towards a disaster.

The apartment in Montrouge seemed smaller than before. Everything was dusty. We all helped clean up, even my father.

The neighborhood was also different, drab and somber. There were no street lights at night.

German soldiers were everywhere. They were not as nice with people as the soldiers who greeted us in Argentan. When they went into a store or a café or anywhere and people were in their way they would push them aside. They would often stop people in the streets to check their identity cards. Trucks full of soldiers were rushing all over the city.

Once in a while, a group of soldiers would walk in step down our street, their rifles on their shoulders, their heavy boots clanking on the pavement, and sing military songs. People would watch them from behind their closed curtains.

There was a curfew. Nobody was allowed in the street in the evening. And when people turned on the lights in their apartments, they had to cover the windows with blankets. Very often there were alerts. The sirens would blare, and everybody would rush down to the cellars.

Though Paris had been declared an Open City and would not be bombed, British planes would bomb the factories in the

suburbs and the trains and military convoys approaching the city. So during the alerts the people would crowd into small cellars with flashlights or candles. My mother would keep us close to her, but my father often refused to go down to the cellar.

All the food was rationed. Once a week mother would go to the *mairie* to get our food stamps. Children were divided into three categories depending on their age, J1, J2, J3. My older sister Sarah was a J3. Jacqueline and I were J2s. That meant that mother was given a few more food stamps for the children. Many people who had money would buy extra food on the black market.

Leon and Marie, who returned to Montrouge before we did, bought a lot of food on the black market. Once in a while aunt Marie would come up to our place and give my mother some extra food, a few eggs, a piece of meat, some sugar, chocolate, *pour les enfants*, she would say. But even with that extra food I was hungry all the time.

Soon after we returned, I started school again. But even school was different. The games we played were not as much fun. We often went home directly after school rather than play in the street. Besides carrying my school bag, I also had to carry a gas mask. Everybody had to carry a gas mask everywhere they went. Sometimes in our apartment my sisters and I would put on our gas masks just for the fun of it, but mother would immediately tell us to put them back into the canister. That's what that metallic case was called.

My sister Sarah started working in a factory. I think it was a factory where they made lampshades. My father also got a job drawing models for a clothing manufacturer. He stayed home more than before. He did the drawings on the dining room table. Only once in a while would he go out to play cards at

the Metropole Café, but he would come home early, before the curfew.

One day he was arrested for having participated in some political gathering. We thought we would never see him again. I remember my mother frantically rushing to the police station to find out what had happened. By that time a lot of men, even married men, were being sent to Germany to work in factories. But he stayed in jail only one day. He was sent home because he had tuberculosis. This was the time when all the Jews had to declare themselves. As I said earlier, because we lived in a suburb where there were only a few Jews, my father decided that we should not declare ourselves. But the anti-Semite in our building denounced us, and my parents had to go to the *préfecture* to declare their identities and their possessions as Jews. And so did Leon and Marie.

Soon after that my mother had to sew the yellow star on all our clothes. I could still go to school, but no longer to swimming pools, museums, libraries, cinemas, and other public places.

It was now the beginning of 1942, according to the newspapers and the radio, the Germans were winning the war. But the people who had a radio would listen quietly to the Free French Radio from London, and even though the emissions were all garbled they would hear that it was the British and the Americans, who were now also in the war, who were winning. It gave people a little hope, even though our daily life was getting more and more difficult and sad.

By now Jewish children were no longer allowed to go to school. So I stayed home. I didn't feel like playing with my tin soldiers. I was too old for that. Nor with my stamp collection. I had reread all my Jules Verne. I would stand at the open window and watch the birds fly, or else count how many people in the street walked past our house, or how many cars

would go by. Sometimes Maman would come and stand next to me and say, Soon the war will be finished, you'll see, the Americans are going to win the war for us, and you'll be able to go to a *lycée,* and then she would put her arm around me and squeeze me, but I would pull away from her.

Things were bad now. Jews were not allowed to take the metro. So we walked wherever we had to go. But mostly we stayed home. Since we didn't own a radio we could not listen to the news. Five of us lived in the same space, but separately from one another. Leon and Marie had a radio, and once in a while my mother would listen to the news with them, especially the news that came from London, and she would tell my father what she had heard. My father still didn't get along with Leon.

By early Spring rumors were circulating that Jewish men were being arrested and sent to labor camps in Germany. Only men.

And then July came. And on the 16th of that month, my childhood ended. After that ...

Federman, very interesting what you just told. Perhaps you should tell more.

I don't think I can, or even want to. It was such a depressing period. And what else is there to say. Everybody lived in fear and sadness.

Alright then, tell us, as you promised in your list, what happened with your cousin Salomon.

I don't know. It's a bit filthy. But since I promised, I suppose should do it.

Sometimes when I was doing my homework and I didn't understand something, especially problems of algebra or geometry, I would ask my cousin Salomon for help.

Salomon was four years older, and he had already studied all that. Besides, everybody in the family said that he was very smart, and gifted in the sciences, and that one day he would certainly become a doctor or a pharmacist. After the war Salomon became a tailor just like his father.

I think Salomon would have preferred to become a gangster. He looked like one of those Chicago gangsters in Hollywood movies. When he was older, and thought himself an adult, he always dressed like a gangster. Double-breasted suit that his father made for him. Salomon always got anything he wanted. So if he wanted a double-breasted suit with stripes, he got it immediately. I think Leon liked when my aunts and uncles complimented him for the new suit he'd made for his son. Salomon was a living model for Leon.

With his gangster suit, Salomon would wear a felt hat with a wide brim pulled down over his eyes when he went out to Montparnasse to meet his friends, who dressed exactly like him. Many of Salomon's buddies had suits made by Leon. In a way, Salomon was like publicity for his father's work. He was good-looking. All the aunts kept telling him how handsome he was. His hair was black and curly. He would slick it back into a duck tail, pulled tight on the sides. He used a lot of brilliantine so his hair would shine and stay in place. Salomon was always so sure of himself. The way he dressed, the way he acted, the way he spoke let people know he was the son of rich parents.

I was so envious of Salomon. Especially of the way he combed his curly hair.

Mine was straight, with a part on the side, and always a bit messy. I didn't take care of my hair. In ***My Body in Nine Parts*** I tell that it was my mother who took care of my hair. She combed it, washed it, made the part on the side, took the lice out of it. She did everything one normally does to hair. After my mother was taken away I had to take care of my own hair. So I became more conscious of how it looked.

After the war, when I returned to Montrouge, I was combing my hair like Salomon, like Marco rather, I should say, since that was the non-Jewish name he gave himself during the war.

Once in a while, after the war, before I left for America, Salomon a.k.a Marco would let me come with him to the Montparnasse cafés where he hung out with his friends. They always called me *Marcotin*, as though I was a diminutive of Marco, but I liked the name.

Let's get back to what happened one day when I went to ask Salomon to help me with my homework.

I go down to his apartment. The door was not locked. I make sure to put my feet on the little *patins* when I go in. Salomon is not in the living room. I look for him in the other rooms, and I find him with his pants at his feet, masturbating in front of the armoire mirror in his parents' bedroom. He didn't get mad when he saw me. He didn't even blush. He turned towards me still holding his erection in his hand and asked, Don't you ever do that?

I didn't answer. I thought he was going to pull his pants up, instead he approached me, still holding his thing in his hand and said, Here suck it for me.

I moved away from him ready to run. I was terrified and embarrassed, but Salomon grabbed the back of my head and pulled me down toward his erection. I resisted even though he was much stronger than me. I struggled, kept pulling back. I even managed to tell him in a kind of sob that if he didn't let me go, I would tell his Father. But he continued to push my head down, and the tip of my nose touched his cock. It gave me a strange sensation. This time I really struggled and managed to escape his grip and I rushed out of the door. Salomon didn't follow me, he just shouted, if you tell my father, you'll pay for it. Keep your mouth shut *petit con.*

I didn't say anything to anyone, but after that I never asked my cousin to help me with my homework. Somehow I managed alone. I was so angry and so scared of him, I avoided him, even in school.

For weeks after that, I kept rubbing my nose with my hand. It was like a tic. I was doing it all the time. My mother would say, Stop doing that. What's wrong with your nose? Does it itch? If you continue like that your nose will be crooked, and all red.

It's true that my nose is big, crooked, and always red. Ah, did my nose make me suffer.

Speaking of my nose, one day in school, when we were studying human anatomy, the teacher, the ugly one, was explaining the different colors of the pigmentation of the skin. She was saying that even among white people there are nuances in the color of the pigment of their skin. For example, she said, pointing to me, *Raymond a le pigment rouge.* And all the boys in the class started laughing and shouting, *Raymond a le piment rouge … Raymond a le piment rouge!*

The word *piment* in French slang means the nose.

The teacher finally managed to stop the laughter. But after that, often in the playground the boys would chant, *Raymond a le pigment rouge … Raymond a le pigment rouge!*

It would make me so angry. But there was nothing I could do about my red nose. And besides, both winter and summer, it was always running. So in school besides being called *fils-de-tubard*, I was also called *petit morveux*.

I had snot coming out of my nose all the time. And when I didn't have a handkerchief, I would wipe my nose with my sleeve. My left sleeve.

I don't remember if I mentioned that I was born left-handed, and became right-handed after I broke my left arm when I fell off a tree. It happened during *les colonies de vacances dans le Poitou*. I fell from a cherry tree. I must have been seven or eight years old.

I wrote quite a bit about my nose in **My Body in Nine Parts,** and also told why I became right-handed. So no need to go into that again. But I do want to add a few things about my hair and how ...

Federman, damn right you've said enough about your nose. Your big crooked nose is everywhere in your writing. And the same about your broken arm, and how you became ambidextrous, and also about your scars, and all the rest.

But that's what marked my childhood. These are the marks that you never forget while all the rest vanishes into the inexpressible. Ah, my nose. As I once put it, a Jewish nose is a little tragedy. In my case, it was more a tragicomedy.

Alright, I'll stop talking about my nose, but I'd like to return a moment to my hair.

In school I often caught lice. When my mother saw me scratching my head, she would say, Come here so I can comb those out of your hair.

She would use a special lice-comb with tight little teeth, and she would comb my hair hard. I would cry that it hurt, and when she pulled the comb of my hair it was full of lice. I remember well now how she would crush them on the comb with her fingernail. She did the same thing with my sisters when they too caught lice in school, but I seemed to always have more lice than them even though they had more hair.

Besides lice there were other little vermin in our house. Bed bugs. Huge cockroaches in the kitchen. And even mice. But no rats. The rats stayed in the cellar.

In the morning if I had been bitten by bed bugs, and I was scratching myself, my mother would rub my body with alcohol.

My father when he saw cockroaches in the kitchen would crush them with his shoes, and then he would tell me to pick up the yellowish goo that came out of the cockroaches and I would throw it into the garbage. That *bouillie* that came out of the crushed cockroaches looked like sperm. It was disgusting.

To catch the mice, my father would set a spring trap with a little piece of bread or cheese in it. He placed it next to the wall where the mice were hiding, and in the morning if there was a dead mouse in the trap, he would tell me to take it out. But I would start crying because I was so scared to touch the mouse. So my father would take it out of the trap holding it by the tail and swing it before my face. My sisters would mock me and would called me *petit trouillard*, and me ...

Federman, do you really need to tell us all that. The snot that came out of your nose, the lice, the bed-bugs, the cockroaches, the mice. Do you think your readers will like that?

I'm not going to censor my childhood just to please the readers. What I am telling here is historical. That's how we lived in those days. In the 1930's. I say it as it was.

Besides, these little beasts were not only in our house. It was like that in all the houses in Montrouge, and I am sure also in all the houses in France. Especially those of poor people. That's why what I just told is historical.

If it offends the readers, let them read something else. The charming novels of La Comtesse de Ségur.

The only little animals I liked were the birds that landed on the window ledges. They were sparrows, I think. I would leave bread crumbs on the ledge and watch from behind the curtain not to scare them. I wanted so much to be able to fly like them. Maybe that's why years later in America, I volunteered for the paratroopers during the Korean war. Just to be in the sky. But that's another story.

I would have liked to have been a bird. Except that in the winter, when it was very cold outside and it snowed, I could imagine how the poor birds were suffering. They were lined up next to each other on electric wires or on the leafless branches of trees. I would ...

Federman, this time you did it. Here you are, sinking into sentimentality. You were warned.

I love birds. Why can't I allow myself a bit of sentimentality about birds? When I lived In New York, I had a friend who was a bird. A pigeon. I called him Charlot. He had only one leg. I told about him in **Smiles on Washington Square.**

Yes, we know. So forget the birds and tell us something else.

Alright then, I'll tell how I once stole a ring in a department store.

I admit it. I confess. I was a bit of a thief when I was a boy. Not a big thief, but I would steal candies in the candy store, pencils and erasers in the stationary store, cigarettes from my father's pack, and once money from my uncle Leon. I think I've already told that I had seen him hide money under the mattress of his bed.

Once in a while, when my aunt Marie knew that my mother didn't have enough money to buy food to feed her children, she would have my sisters and I come and eat with them. One day, we were all sitting at the dining room table, my uncle Leon, my cousin Salomon, and my sisters, when aunt Marie told me to go get more bread from the kitchen. To get to the kitchen I had to go through their bedroom. So quickly, before going into the kitchen, I reached under the mattress and pulled out a bill, and without looking at it I shoved it in my pocket. Later, in the bathroom I took it out to see how much it was. It was a twenty franc bill. With that money I bought myself some stamps for my collection and a fountain pen. Still to this day, I love having fountain pens.

When my father saw this new pen, he asked where I got it, and I told him that Salomon gave it to me because he had many of them. My father didn't say anything. But I was afraid that he would guess that I had lied. I think I turned all red when I answered him.

Yes, I was a bit of a liar as a boy. But all little boys are liars and sneaky, even if ....

And now, Federman, you're not a liar anymore? Who are you trying to kid?

Well, let's say that now I know how to invent better.

My biggest crime was when I stole a ring in a department store.

In school most of the boys my age had a ring. A ring with a skull on it. When you put ink on the skull and pressed it on a sheet of paper it would make human skulls.

I wanted so much to have a ring like that, but I didn't have money to buy one. The few centimes my parents gave me once in a while I spent buying stamps for my collection or tin soldiers, and sometimes candy. My mother always said that I was a gourmand when I was a boy. But I wanted to have a ring with a skull on it.

One day when I was coming home from an errand, I stopped at the *Monoprix*, a store that sold all kinds of things. I just wanted to look. And I see that they were selling rings with skulls on them. I looked at them a while. I even touched one. A big one, the color of silver. The lady behind the counter had moved away to help somebody else. I looked around. Nobody was paying attention to me. Quickly I closed my hand on the ring and moved away from the counter my hand still closed. I walked around the store pretending to be looking at things. I was very nervous and scared. Then I put my hand in my pocket and dropped the ring inside. I looked around. Still, no one was paying attention to me. The store was crowded with customers and the sales ladies were busy with them. Slowly I walked toward the exit. Suddenly a man wearing a grey suit grabbed me by the arm and said, Come with me, you little thief. I saw you. And he pulled me to the back of the store. I didn't resist, but I felt my legs trembling under me. I was on the verge of tears, but I held back.

We were now in a little room in the back of the store. A bare room except for a table and one chair. Another man came in. He also wore a suit, a black one.

I have never forgotten their suits. The suits were what scared me the most. I thought these men were policemen in civilian clothes.

The man who caught me explains that he saw me stealing a ring which I put in my pocket. The man in black tells me to empty my pockets on the table in front of me. I don't move. I'm frozen in place.

Empty your pocket, he shouts, or I will do it for you.

It was a summer day. I was wearing a short sleeve shirt, a pair of shorts, and sandals. I put my hand in my pockets and took out what was inside. A handkerchief, not too clean, a little pencil stub, a used eraser, two centimes, and the ring.

Ah, ah, the man in the grey suit says, while shaking me by the arm and pointing to the ring on the table. You see, I was right, he tells the man in black, that little thief stole that ring.

The man in black asks me why I stole that ring, and I answered, without thinking, without hesitating, that tomorrow is my mother's birthday and I wanted to give her a present, but I don't have any money.

That's exactly what I said. I swear. It came out of me just like that. I had to invent something.

The two men remained silent, but I saw on their faces that they had a little smile. After a moment, that felt like an eternity, the man in the black suit asked me to write my name and my address on a piece of paper. I had to. So I wrote my real name and my real address. It didn't occur to me to write a false name and a false address. I was thinking, they are going to send the police to my house and arrest me. My father is going to kill me. My mother will be so ashamed of me.

After having examined what I had written, the man in black said, Okay, go home. We'll decide what to do.

So I left. While walking home, I was terribly worried about what would happen when the police would come to arrest me.

The next day, when school was over, I didn't dare go home. I imagined my parents waiting for me, and asking for an explanation.

Several days passed. And each time, before going home after school, I was trembling with fear in the street. But nobody came.

I never told this to anyone. No even to my friend Bébert, who like me also stole candy and others thing in stores, and even cigarettes from his father which we smoked together.

Well, as you can see, I was not a great criminal, but maybe a bit of a pervert. Let me explain.

When I was old enough to take the subway alone sometimes when there was no school and the boys who played soccer in the street didn't let me play with them because they said I didn't know how to play, I would take the subway to the station *St. Paul* in *le Marais* to visit my aunt Ida, my father's youngest sister whom he adored, and whom I also liked because she was always nice to me. There I would play with my cousins Simon and Raymond, the younger one had the same name as me, and also with my little cousin Sarah who was so cute and whom I loved very much.

My cousin Sarah is the only survivor of her family. For the past sixty years she's been living in Israel. I told her story in **To Whom it May Concern.**

I would play with Sarah and her two brothers in the garden of Place des Vosges. The same Place des Vosges where the *Grand-Rafle* took place. The beautiful Place des Vosges with its arcades, its garden, its fountain, its chestnut trees, and Victor Hugo's house. I loved to read the plaque on that house that said that Victor Hugo lived there from 1832 to 1848. I had learned many of his poems by heart in school, and looking at his house made me feel close to him. As if I knew him personally. I would wonder what I would have to do later in life to have a plaque like this on my house in Montrouge.

It was at this time, when I was old enough to take the subway alone, that I started looking at women. The boys in school often told each other stories about women while giggling.

One day when we were playing Place des Vosges, my cousin Simon said to me, Come with me. I want to show you something.

So we left Sarah and Raymond, and we walked to rue St. Denis. The famous rue St. Denis. It's there that I saw prostitutes for the first time. I asked Simon what these women standing in the street or in doorways were doing there. Why they were waiting like that. And why all these *messieurs* were going inside the houses with them. And my cousin laughed.

You don't know what a *putain* is?

No, I didn't know. So my cousin explained what these women were doing.

Even though Simon was my age, he seemed to know a lot of things I didn't know.

I asked him if he ever went with one of these beautiful women in very short skirts and black stockings, and who kept asking us as we walked past them, *Tu montes, mon petit chéri.* Come on little love, I'll do nice things to you.

Are you mad, my cousin answered, it costs a lot of money to go with them. And besides you could catch a disease.

After that, whenever I went to visit aunt Ida, or my other aunts who lived in the Marais, I would get off the subway at the station Châtelet and make a detour to rue St. Denis. Now that I knew what a prostitute was, I would blush when one of the beautiful women would ask me to go with them. I never dared.

Federman, don't tell me you never fucked a prostitute.

Yes, in Tokyo when I was in the army, but this has nothing to do with my childhood. So no need to go into that.

Instead I want to tell something else. Something important. How I got from Montrouge to Monflanquin after I came out of the closet. I've never told that story. The end of a childhood.

The End of a Childhood

I have never told how I went from the closet to the farm. How I got from Montrouge to Monflanquin when I finally emerged from the hole into which my mother had hidden me, and where my childhood vanished into the dark.

This crucial moment of my survival, this emergence from the tomb-womb into the light and into life has remained so vague in the stories I've told for so many years.

Perhaps it's because I told so many different versions, all so nebulous, to the point that I myself don't even know which is the true version, or if there is one, the real story of what happened after I came out of the closet with a smelly package of shit in my hands which I left on the roof of our house before tip-toeing down the stairs, and then frantically running into the street towards the enigma of my future days of deportation to the farm

This wandering in a no-man's-land between Montrouge and Mont-flanquin lasted six days, during which I was lost in incomprehension. Oblivious to what was happening to me and around me.

In **Return to Manure** I tell how the boy of that story jumped from a freight train that was racing south in *La Zone Libre* towards he knew not where, and how he landed into a muddy ditch, and how all bloodied and bruised he asked an old farmer working in the fields which way to Montflanquin, and the old farmer seemingly unconcerned by the boy's condition pointed towards the west and mumbled, *vingt kilomètres* *tout droit dans cette direction*, and how dragging a wounded leg, the boy followed his shadow to the little town of Monflanquin where Leon, Marie, and Salomon had taken refuge before the round-up, and how surprised they were to see him, for they were convinced that, like his parents and sisters, he was already on his way to his final solution, and how to get rid of this unexpected burden they exchanged him for two chickens to a farm woman in need of help to do the farm work because her husband was a prisoner in Germany. No need to tell all that again.

As I come to the end of the story of my childhood, I would like to tell what happened during these six days of wandering.

I have an idea. I'm going to tell that story in the form of a time-table. This way it'll go faster.

About 5:30 a.m. on July 16, 1942, the French police who were doing the dirty work of the Gestapo—*les j'ai ta peau*, as the poet Max Jacob called those who deported him—came to arrest us, *au 4 Rue Louis Rolland à Montrouge*, because we were Jewish. Undesirable.

It was then that my mother pushed me into a closet on the landing of our apartment, on the third floor, and quietly shut the door behind me as she murmured *Chut*.

About 6:00 a.m. the next day, I finally came out of the closet after having spent an entire day and night in that closet.

About 7:00 a.m. on July 17, 1942., I walked from Montrouge to Rue des Francs-Bourgeois in Le Marais where my aunt Ida and her husband

Aaron lived with their three children, Simon, Raymond, and Sarah. I tell them breathlessly what happened, how the police came to arrest us, how my mother hid me in a closet. It took me a good hour to get to where they lived. I walked as fast as I could trying not to be noticed by the

policemen and the German soldiers who were everywhere in the streets. I could not take the subway because when I came out of the closet I had nothing, nothing except the shirt, the shorts and *espadrilles* my mother had shoved into my arms. I had no money, no subway tickets, no food stamps. I had nothing except my fear.

Still breathing hard from the long walk, I tell my aunt and uncle that they must leave immediately before the police arrive. I tell them the streets are full of policemen and German soldiers arresting people. My uncle Aaron tells me that they don't know where to go, they don't know anybody who will hide them, and besides they don't have money to buy train tickets. So they are hoping nobody will come. But they have already packed their little bundles.

All the Jews in this neighborhood know that the *Rafle* is in progress. It started very early the day before. While my uncle tells me that they don't know what to do, my aunt Ida is cowering in a corner of the room softly crying while holding her two sons close to her. My cousin Sarah is not there.

In **To Whom It May Concern** I told the ~~dolorous~~ story of how my little cousin Sarah survived. The only one from her family.

A few minutes after 7:00 a.m., the same day, my aunt Ida tells me and Simon, the oldest of her two sons, to go quickly see if aunt Basha is still at home. Maybe she's still asleep and has no idea what is going on. Basha always sleeps late, and besides she's unaware of what is going on in the world.

Aunt Basha was my father's oldest sister. She lived at the corner of Rue Beaubourg and Rue Rambuteau. A five minute walk from Rue des Francs-Bourgeois.

I should specify that aunt Basha's husband, Ruben, and her two sons, Raymond and Roger, had left Paris before *La Grande Rafle*. A rumor had been circulating for days that only men would be arrested. So aunt Basha stayed in her apartment to protect their possessions. Ruben was a wealthy tailor. She felt secure staying in her apartment. After all she was a French citizen even though she barely could speak French. Yiddish was her language.

About 7:15 a.m., still the same day, having climbed the six flights of stairs to aunt Basha's apartment, my cousin and I explain to her what is happening.

Aunt Basha bursts into Yiddish lamentations and keeps repeating *Oy Vey Oy Veys Mirh!* while dragging a big suitcase out of a closet and frantically shoving into it, not clothing, but silver objects, jewelry, documents and handfuls of large bills that she pulls out from under the mattress. She carefully locks her apartment, and we rush down the stairs, Simon and I struggling with the big suitcase, while behind us aunt Basha is puffing and mumbling more *Oy Vey Oy Vey,* and telling us to hurry up. Outside in the street, aunt Basha waves to a taxi going by, she shoves a bill in the hand of the driver as she explains in her broken French where she wants to go. Simon and I push the suitcase into the back seat of the cab. Aunt Basha climbs in, slams the door close, and the taxi speeds away. Through the back window of the taxi our aunt Basha waves to us leaving us baffled on the sidewalk.

I have never understood what that waving gesture meant.

Not much more to say about this scene. I have settled my account with aunt Basha in ***To Whom It May Concern***.

Federman, do you really need to elaborate that much? Didn't your old friend Sam once say, less is more, and that we must seek fundamental sounds?

Yeah, yeah, I know, I'm trying to say less, but I have to finish telling how my childhood came to an end.

The only thing I want to add here, is that at the very place where aunt Basha's apartment building stood, the Beaubourg Museum of Modern Art was built. Right there, at the corner of Rue Rambuteau and Rue Beaubourg. What a colorful substitution. The immorality of history replaced by the insolence modern art.

About 7:30, still the same morning, back to my aunt Ida's apartment. The police are there. One of the policemen asks which of us is Simon Bialek. My cousin points to himself. The policeman asks who I am. My Aunt Ida quickly says that I am a friend of her son's, but not Jewish.

It is true that when I came out of the closet I had the presence of mind to tear the yellow star off my shirt.

The policeman asks my name. Hesitantly I say Federman. He looks at his list, and then tells me I can go. My name is not on his list. He explains that he can take only those people whose names are on his list, If we take just anybody that will cause all kinds of bureaucratic problems, we have enough problems already finding all the people who have to be moved out. Even though he says I could go, I stay. The policemen don't seem to mind. They are doing their job.

I walk along with my aunt, my uncle and my two cousins and the policemen to Place des Vosges. On the way, my aunt keeps whispering to me that I should go away. *Va-ten! Va-ten! Sauve-toi!* She pleads in my ear. But I want to see where they are being taken. Perhaps my parents and sisters will be there, and I can join them.

Big army trucks with canvas covers are stationed around the entire periphery of the square. People escorted by policemen are pouring into the Place des Vosges from all directions. They all have a yellow star on their clothing and are carrying small suitcases or bundles. Even though it is summer, many are wearing overcoats. Some even have blankets with them. It's like a gathering of people going on vacation to a cold place. There is no screaming, no shouting, but people have tears in their eyes.

It was on that historic Place des Vosges, that I kissed my aunt, my uncle, and my two cousins before they were pushed up into a truck crowded with frightened faces.

Before getting on the truck, my cousin Simon showed me the little pocket knife he had with him. It could be useful where we're going, he said.

About 8:00 a.m., still on July 17, 1942, the trucks roared out of Place des Vosges leaving behind a trail of dark smoke. I stood there for a while, unable to move, wondering why I was not in one of those trucks. Who had made that decision? Who had chosen me?

No, I am not going to fall for that divine intervention crap. And I'm sure that the boy that I was then didn't think of that. His mind was a blob of confusion. It is I, more than sixty years later, who continues to wonder why me? Why was I left standing on that square?

I stood there a long time. No one was paying attention to me. It was as though I had become invisible.

About 9:00 a.m., still the same day, I walked all the way back to Montrouge. I had convinced myself that my parents and sisters were back in our apartment. That they had been sent home. That they were waiting for me. Worrying about me. I imagined my mother looking into the closet to see if I was still there.

Walking at a frantic pace, I am replaying in my head what happened since my mother closed the door. Everything was so confused, so incomprehensible. Especially the fact that the policeman who asked my name did not react when I said Federman.

Federman, such a good Jewish name. And with my big crooked nose and my biddy dark eyes I look like such a *Youpin*. Maybe the policeman noticed that, but ... But what?

Could it be that he thought, at least one of them will be saved?

The other day, when I told my lovely daughter Simone that I felt more French than Jewish, she said with her typical federmanesque humor: Pop, your circumcision is written all over your face.

About 9:10 a.m., hidden behind a tree in our street, I observe our house. I don't dare go into the building because of the people on the main floor. The wooden blinds of our apartment on the third floor are shut. Also those of aunt Marie and uncle Leon's apartment. But theirs were like that already a few days ago. They closed their apartment and left several days before *La Grande Rafle*. I stay hidden behind for a while. The street is deserted. I don't know where to go.

Suddenly I remember that a woman who used to wash people's laundry at the public *lavoir* with my mother lives down the street. She was not a friend of my mother, but she was a nice lady, they often talked about how difficult life was. Maybe she knows where my parents were taken.

Maybe she can tell me what to do.

About 9:20 a.m, I knock on her door. She opens and seems surprised to see me, I suppose because everyone in the neighborhood must know by now what happened the day before. She looks furtively down the stairs and pulls me by

the arm into her apartment. I tell her how my mother hid me in a closet when the police came, where I stayed all day yesterday until this morning. The tears are in my throat while telling her. She asks if I am hungry. I say yes. She gives me a piece of bread and a glass of milk. She seems concerned. I suppose she doesn't know what to do with me. Her husband who works in a factory will certainly be furious when he sees me. She told my mother on many occasions that her husband beat her. The woman asks if I was seen going into her building. I say, I don't think so. She goes to the window several times to look down the street.

About 9:45 a.m., the woman says to me, I have an idea, you know what we're going to do? I'm going to take you to the *commissariat de police*, and there they'll know where your parents and sisters are, and they'll put you with them. I don't see any problem with that. Besides, I'm sure your family will be sent home soon.

So about 10:00 a.m., I'm walking towards the Montrouge police station with this woman holding my hand. Suddenly, abruptly I pull my hand away from hers and start running in the opposite direction, away from the police station. I hear the woman shouting behind me, Come back, come back, don't run away. They'll catch you. I keep running.

Still on July 17, 1942, I wander aimlessly in the streets of Montrouge, far from where we live. All is calm now. All the Jews in Montrouge have been taken away. I am afraid to go back to Rue Louis Rolland, so I'll wait until after dark to go see if there is light in our apartment. When I see a policeman and some German soldiers, I quickly go inside the doorway of a building.

Tired of walking, I sit on a bench in a public park. Children are playing. Mothers are gossiping while knitting. I almost fall

asleep, sitting up. I am still hungry. When it starts to get dark, I walk back to our house. The blinds of our apartment are still closed. No light. I now know that my parents have not return. I must leave Paris. But go where? How?

I go to *La Gare Montparnasse* to see if I can sneak on a train. Any train going anywhere, away from the city. I know that's what I must do. I heard my mother often say, If we had the money I would get on a train and take the children to Monflanquin. They would be safe with Maurice. But of course, we never had enough money to ...

No need to speculate. At least, I knew then, that somehow I must try to reach the Free Zone.

Even though it's late in the evening, the train station is full of policemen and German soldiers. I am afraid to go into the departure hall. I wander in the streets around the train station. It's very late now. Everything is dark in the city. All the stores are closed. And there are no lights in the windows of the buildings. People have closed the shutters or used blankets to cover the windows, so the light wouldn't be seen. The streets are deserted. It's the curfew.

Hard to remember what time it was when I tried to fall asleep curled up on the floor in the corridor of a building whose entrance door had not been locked. I was no longer afraid of darkness. The night was protecting me.

I must have fallen asleep when a man who was coming home late, in spite of the curfew, woke me by kicking me in the leg and shouting, What the hell are you doing here, *petit voyou*! Get out of here!

I found another unlocked door, and again I curled up on the floor of the corridor, but I couldn't sleep. I was hungry. I didn't know what I was going to do in the morning. I was afraid to go back to the station because of the policemen and the soldiers.

As soon as it was light outside, I walked back to Montrouge. It was as though something was pulling me there, still hoping that my parents and sisters had been sent home. The blinds of our apartment were still shut.

About 7:00 a.m July 18th, I go back to the Gare Montparnasse. Maybe this time I can sneak on a train.

The station is crowded with people, regular travelers, but not as many policemen and German soldiers. The round-up must be over. I'm determined to get on a train going in any direction.

I study the train schedule. No one is paying attention to me. When I see a policeman or a German soldier coming towards me, I stand next to someone as if I were with that person. Next to a woman with children, pretending that I am one of her children.

Several trains are leaving that morning, but I notice that policemen and German soldiers are checking people's papers and tickets as they board the trains. I am afraid to try sneaking on. I go into the waiting room. I don't know what to do. I feel like bursting into tears. I go back out into the departure hall to see if there is a way I can get on one of the trains. It looks impossible. I go back to the waiting room. I sit there in a corner for hours. In the toilet I drink some water from the faucet. Late in the afternoon two young men walk in and sit on a bench across from me. They are not much older than me. I walk up to them. I need to talk to someone. They look friendly. They ask me what I'm doing here, alone.

Even though I don't know who they are, I tell them everything that happened in the past two days. I tell them that I have no money and that I am trying to sneak on a train to get away from Paris. They tell me they want to do the same thing.

But not in a passenger train, they explain, because the police and the Germans inspect all the trains. They are going to try to sneak onto a freight train. In fact, they tell me, they have already picked out a freight train that will leave for the south of France later that evening. For the free zone, they explain. I ask them if I can go with them. They say yes. But we'll have to be careful, and quick to get on that train after it has been inspected.

The two young men tell me that they come from Belgium, and that they are trying to get to Spain, and from there to North Africa to join the free forces of General de Gaulle. They are both eighteen years old.

Not to attract too much attention we decide to go for a walk outside the station. Both young men carry a small backpack. We walk around, but not far from the station. One of the young men asks if I'm hungry. I tell him, I haven't eaten for two days, except for a piece of bread and a glass of milk. I had told them about the lady who wanted to take me to the police.

He opens his backpack and takes out a piece of bread and some salami, and gives it to me. He explains that they cannot go into a grocery store to buy food because they don't have food tickets for French stores. And besides, they don't have much money. So they brought some food with them. I thank them, and I eat the bread and salami while we continue to walk.

Finally when it's starting to get dark we go back into the station. There are fewer people now, and less policemen and soldiers too. OK, let's go the young men say. The train is leaving soon. It has already been inspected. Together we

quickly sneak on the side of the train which it not along the loading platform. We slide open the big door of one of the cars, and we climb in. The car is full of large wooden crates. We hide between them. We can hear voices outside. We crouch further between the boxes. Someone closes the door on the side of the platform. We made it. The two young men smile at me, while holding a finger over their mouths.

About 11:00 p.m. the train starts rolling slowly, and then gains speed. Soon we are out of the city.

The young men open their backpack and take out sandwiches made of meat and cheese, and a bottle of water. Together we eat and drink. From time to time one of the young men slides the door slightly open to see where we are. According to the names of the stations the train is passing without stopping, we are traveling Southwest, towards *La Zone Libre*. That's what the young men tell me. This means that before arriving to the border that separates the occupied zone from the free zone, we'll have to get off this train, otherwise we'll be caught. All the trains crossing into the free zone are being inspected by the Germans. We'll have to get off before.

One of the young men takes a little flashlight and a map of France out of his bag, and studies it. According to the names of the stations we have already passed, the train will probably stop at the Vierzon station to be inspected. That's where the line of demarcation is. If the train does not stop at a station before that, we will have to jump while the train is still rolling.

Don't worry. Don't be afraid, the young men tell me. We'll take care of you. We'll wait till the train slows down around a curve, and we'll show you how to jump and roll on the ground.

I'll be about another two hours before Vierzon. Why don't you get some sleep the young men tell me.

I don't remember the name of these young men, but I will never forget them. I felt secure with them. I felt like a younger brother.

About 2:30 in the middle of the night, by chance the train stops in the middle of nowhere. The two young men study their maps. We are about ten kilometers from Vierzon. Let's get off here, they say. We'll hide somewhere, and tomorrow, during the night we'll walk to the Vierzon station to see if we can get across the line of demarcation. We may have to sneak onto another train, they explain. Again they tell me not to worry. Not to be scared. I tell them I'm not scared.

Not far from where the train stopped we come upon an old abandoned barn in the middle of a field. We settle in.

One of the young men goes out to see if he can find something to eat. He comes back with some raw potatoes and turnips. That's all he could find. We rub the dirt from these and eat them raw. If no one comes to the barn in the morning, we'll stay there all day, and then at night we'll walk to the Vierzon station to study the situation. Hopefully in the morning we can find some better food in the fields. Maybe even some fruit. After having eaten the potatoes and turnips, I fall asleep on a pile of hay.

We remained hidden in the barn the entire following day. No one came. One of us stood guard, while the other two slept.

The young man who found the potatoes and turnips went back out into the fields looking for more food. This time he came back with some carrots and peaches. He also said that not far from the barn there was a little stream. The three of us went there to drink some fresh water and wash our faces.

I was already starting to forget what happened these past few days. Everything seemed to have vanished from my mind. I

felt protected by these two young men. I hadn't told them that I had decided to go all the way to Africa with them, but already I saw myself fighting with De Gaulle's free forces. Even if I was only a boy, I could be useful. I would be like a mascot.

Having fought many battles with my tin soldiers, maybe General de Gaulle might even let me carry a rifle to fight in the war against the Germans.

About 1:00 a.m. in the middle of the night, on July 20th, after having walked the ten kilometers to Vierzon, one of the young men goes to scout the situation at the train station, while the other young man and I stay hidden in a ditch.

From where we are we can see what is going on at the station. Workers are loading freight trains while being watched by German soldiers.

About 1:15 a.m. the young man comes back and tells us that it will not be easy. There are too many soldiers everywhere inspecting all the trains. He doesn't think we can get on a train tonight. We'll try again tomorrow.

We go back to the old abandoned barn, and spend the entire day there. To be sure that no one comes, again one of us stands guard while the other two sleep. I take my turn. I already feel like a real soldier. When it's night we walk again to the Vierzon station.

It's about 3:00 a.m. in the morning on July 21st. We've been observing the station for a long time. Like the night before workers are busy loading material on freight trains watched by German soldiers. It would be too dangerous to try to get on one of these trains tonight, even after it's loaded. We'll have to come back tomorrow. Maybe it won't be so busy. Or we'll have to find another way to cross into the free zone.

We are about to go back to our refuge when suddenly we hear loud sirens, and we see all the workers and the soldiers too run in the same direction. All the lights go out. What a stroke of luck, the young men say. It's an alert. They're all going to the bomb shelters. There must be British planes coming. Let's go. We jump out of the ditch where we were hiding and run towards the train that the workers were loading. We see other people carrying suitcases also running towards the train. They were hiding in a shack in the middle of the tracks. These were people who had payed the *passeurs* to get across the line of demarcation. We climb into one of the cars.

About 3:20 a.m., same night, we hear the sirens again. The workers and soldiers come out of the shelters. It seems that it was a false alert. Or maybe it was a fake alert to allow the people who had payed the *passeurs* to get on the train. In any case, we have made it too.

The car in which we are hiding is full of bales of wire. We hear voices outside, but since this car was already inspected we feel safe. The door on the side of the platform is already closed.

About 3:30 a.m. on July 21st, the train starts rolling. Five minutes later, one of the young men slides the door of the car open and says, we are in *La Zone Libre*. The three of us stand at the door looking out, the wind blowing in our faces. The train is now going full speed. The smoke of the engine fills our car.

The two young men keep consulting their maps each time the train speeds past a sleepy train station. Several hours later one of them exclaims we are in le Lot-et-Garonne, just past Bergerac. The Lot-et-Garonne, I exclaim. I have an uncle who lives in this part of the country.

I tell them that my uncle Maurice, who was called into the army when the war started, was in the Dunkirk debacle, and after he escaped from the German army he took refuge in the free zone in a little town called Montflanquin.

They ask me how I know that. I explain that my uncle Leon and my aunt Marie, a sister of my mother, who lived in the same building with us, often told the story of how my uncle Maurice escaped and took refuge in Montflanquin where his wife Nenette managed to join him by paying some *passeur* to get across the line of demarcation. I am almost sure that this is also where my uncles and aunts who left before *La Grande Rafle* must be. In fact, they were there still alive, I discovered when I finally made it to Montflanquin.

I tell the young men that I think I'm going to jump off the train and try to find my family. So they look on their map to find Montflanquin, but they can't. Doesn't matter, I tell them. I'm going to jump here anyway. I am sure I can find that town, and my uncles and aunts will take care of me. The Lot-et-Garonne mustn't be too big. And maybe I'll be lucky and jump not too far from Montflanquin.

About 6:00 a.m. on July 21, 1942, when the train slowed down around a sharp curve, I said goodbye to my two friends and jumped from the train. I landed in a deep muddy ditch. When I climbed out of that ditch I was all muddied. I had hurt my knee. And my nose was bleeding. But I was still alive.

The rest of this story is told in **Return to Manure**. As for the great adventures I could have had in Africa with these two young men, they were now all but forgotten.

Well, that's the story of those few days of wandering during which my childhood vanished behind me. At least, that's what I'm able to reconstruct from the holes in my memory. Perhaps next time I'll remember another version.

Federman when will you finally tell the real story of what happened to you after you came out of the closet. All that sounds so invented.

It is invented. Well, it's re-invented. It had to be. Do you think that I lived all my life preserving the details of this adventure.

The only thing I know for sure is that soon after my arrival in Montflanquin, I started working on a farm. I admit that how I got there still remains blurry in my mind.

Federman, to tell one's childhood, one's life, demands an honest participation with memory. The stories you are telling, even if you deform them, are souvenirs that you have kept in you. Don't you feel a sense of responsibility towards them? Don't you feel responsible for their veracity?

Don't come and bug me with this question of responsibility and of duty to memory. Le devoir à la mémoire.

Me, totally amoral as I am, lost in my head, me who should have changed tense a long time ago, how can I be responsible towards what I write? What do I owe to memory?

Responsible writing is always false, because responsibility is a lie. One believes oneself responsible, but in fact one is only pretending to be.

Those who exterminated my family believe themselves to be responsible for cleansing humanity of a vermin—Ungeziefer.

And why should one have a sense of duty towards one's souvenirs? As if one owes them something. A tax. A debt that must be repaid.

209

To remember is to play a mental cinema that falsifies the original event. Souvenirs are fiction.

When I write, I don't give a damn about what I owe to memory. Otherwise it would mean that I write to repay what I owe to those who forced me to write. What do I owe them?

Those who have read me up to now will say, he owes his life to his mother. His duty is to repay her.

Yes, that's true. But this mass of words I have left behind, in English, French, Charabia, that's my recompense to her. I have written all that for her, in order to decode the great silence she imposed on me with her CHUT.

My duty, if I must have one, is to fill the hole of absence that my mother dug into me. My duty is to render her absence present. And thus give a little dignity to those whose lives were humiliated.

So now on with the story in Montrouge.

One night, it was winter, we were still all asleep, when suddenly we hear fire engine sirens in the street, and the *Pin Pon* of police cars.

My mother gets up and rushes to the window and shouts, the factory across the street is on fire! My father goes to the window to see. And me too. I squeeze my head between them to look. I see the flames coming out of the windows of the factory and the smoke rising into the sky. Even the trees in front of the factory are burning. People are in the street looking at the firemen who are starting to fight with the fire with long water hoses. The whole scene looks beautiful. It's like a scene in a story. That's what I thought when I saw the fire.

My mother anxiously says, it's dangerous, the fire could cross the street. Come on children get dressed quickly, we have to go down. At that very moment a knock on the door. My father opens it. A policeman tells us that we must evacuate immediately. The fire is spreading in the street from the factory.

My mother takes out a suitcase from the closet to put things in it. The policeman tells her there is no time for that. We must go down immediately before it's too late. When I hear that, I see myself surrounded by fire. I must cross the fire if I want to survive. My sisters and I are not yet fully dressed. I must cross this fire, I'm thinking while getting dressed. You don't have time to finish getting dressed, the policeman says. Just grab your clothes and you'll get dressed in the street. Take blankets with you because it's very cold outside. We don't know yet where we're going to put all the people who are being evacuated.

Mother opens the drawer of the buffet to take her precious silverware, but the policeman tells her leave all that. But she manages to slip it all in a little bag as the policeman pulls her by the arm towards the door.

Father has put on his overcoat over his pyjamas, also a hat, and a long scarf around his neck.

We are rushing now down the dark stairs, each with a blanket over our shoulders.

In front of us in the stairs Leon, Marie and Salomon are also going down. Leon is wearing his robe de chambre and he has a little satchel in his hand. Probably full of the money he hides under the mattress of his bed.

In the street policemen and gendarmes are urging the people to move away from the raging fire. There is heavy smoke everywhere burning our eyes and making us cough. The firemen are hurling water on the fire with their long hoses, but the flames are spreading to the buildings next to the factory.

A police officer on a horse tells the people with a megaphone that they must immediately go take refuge in the school on Rue de Bagneux. My school. Many people resist. They want to see if their homes are going to burn. But the policemen and the gendarmes are forcing them to retreat. The smoke is now unbearable. While walking quickly towards the school, my mother is pulling me by the hand. I would like to stay to see what will happen when all the houses in the street burn. I see myself in another scene. I am lost in a big dark cloud of smoke which I must cross to reach where I am going. Stop dragging your feet, my mother says, the fire is catching us.

My sisters are running in front of us holding hands. My father is somewhere behind us.

I look at all that like a great adventure. I would like our house to burn, this way we could go live somewhere else.

We are now in the school. Ladies with Red Cross uniforms are organizing things. They put groups of people in different rooms. They give coffee to the people and milk to the children.

Our street, Rue Louis Rolland, is now closed at both ends.

Late in the afternoon, *le commissaire de police de Montrouge* comes to the school and tells the assembled refugees that even though the fire is almost completely controlled, no one is allowed to go back home because of the heavy smoke still lingering in the air.

So we have to stay in the school overnight. Merchants from the neighborhood bring food for the people who have been evacuated.

My mother manages to get us double portions of everything because, she tells the people distributing the food, the children have not eaten in two days.

A rumor is circulating that it was the Sidis who set the factory on fire because they were forced to work in such a filthy smelly place. It's true that the terrible stench of the cow hides being remade into leather had disappeared with the fire.

For weeks after the fire was finally extinguished, workers continued to demolish and remove the ruins of the factory. When it was all cleared up, from the windows of our apartment we could see the entire city of Montrouge. It made me feel free. It made me feel like I could fly away. I would open the window and lean way out over the edge, my arms extended like wings and I would pretend that I was flying into the sky. My mother would scream at me, Stop that, you're going to fall. Move back from the window.

That's how the factory in front of our house disappeared. After that, the people were saying that the neighborhood had become less dangerous now that the *Sidis* were no longer working here. In the evening people would walk in the street without fear, and...

Federman, did you just make up this whole thing about the fire just so that you could tell us a little adventure story.

No, the fire really happened. And it's true about the view.

But the following year big ugly apartment buildings were built there, and the view disappeared. Just like that.

Just like that. But my imagining flying out of the window, that was a happy moment.

Oh, I have to tell something else that happened in our neighborhood. Something funny.

One day, or rather one night, Marius's café at the corner of the street was burglarized. It was a big café, with an old zinc bar, and a billiard table in the back. Children were not allowed to go into the café. Except when their parents sent them to by cigarettes. This *bistrot* was for adults who came after work to have a few drinks, and often remained late into the night and would stagger home totally drunk.

The next morning, a Sunday, three police cars arrived full speed with their blaring *Pin Pon Pin Pon* and stopped in front of the café. Everybody in the neighborhood rushed to see what was happening. The policemen explained that during the night burglars broke a window to get into the café, and stole a lot of bottles of liquor, and even some money.

During the burglary, one of the thieves relieved himself on the billiard table. When Marius arrived early in the morning and saw that big load in the middle of his billiard table he almost fainted. But when the policemen saw that, they all laughed, and soon after all the people in the neighborhood knew what had happened, and wanted to see that big pile on Marius' billiard table. People lined up outside the café, and there was such a crowd the policemen had to direct traffic.

They would allow only a dozen people at a time to enter. Outside in the street, people were pushing and shoving like mad to get in. Without the police it would have been a real riot. The policemen kept shouting, Calm down, everybody will get a chance to see. Move along, move along, they would say to the people around the table. A little faster. Don't be selfish. Let the others see. Some people were taking pictures. That day even children were allowed into Marius's café.

Even I went to see, but my sisters refused to go. They said it was disgusting to go see something like that.

Poor Marius. He looked so ashamed. He was sitting at a table in the corner of the café, his head between his hands. He looked like he was crying.

That pile of shit on his billiard table bugged him for the rest of his life. When people came into the café they would ask, Marius how is your big turd? What did you do with it? Did you cook it? Marius became neurasthenic because of this burglary, and barely talked to anyone.

Well, that's enough for that, now I'll tell something else. But before going any further with my stories, I have to decide whether or not I should put here what I wrote to Francesca, a young Italian graduate student who is writing a doctoral dissertation about the bilingual aspect of my work, who asked in a letter how the book I am writing is going, and in which language it is being written.

I don't know if I should put my reply here, in the pages reserved for stories, or in the separate pages of commentaries and arguments.

Well, I'll put it here, I can always displace it later.

Dear Francesca,

I'm on page 217 of a novel I'm writing in English. It's called *Shhh: The Story of a Childhood*.

I say novel, but is it really a novel, in the traditional sense of that word? What I'm writing has no plot. No suspense. No possibility of a resolution. Let's just say that I'm telling stories.

I'm telling, in my usual way, the story of my childhood. The thirteen years that preceded the adventure of the closet.

I say telling, or rather I should say, I'm reconstructing with words what I believe my childhood to have been.

I'm reinventing most of it. I do so, without any respect for chronology, with debris of souvenirs, and fragments of stories I've already told elsewhere. I also do it by inserting poems, mini-stories, quotations, digressions into the text.

I'm telling this childhood in the first person, in a tone perhaps a bit too serious for me. It's dangerous, because such a tone can easily lead to sentimentality.

Fortunately, voices constantly interrupt the narrative by addressing Federman— that's the name of the storyteller—warning him to avoid agonizing realism and decadent lyricism, and especially not to exaggerate too much.

These interruptions, commentaries, arguments, critiques, etc. are presented on separate pages in italics.

It is difficult to tell now where all this will lead me, but I'm progressing, in spite of my deficient memory, in this reconstruction of a childhood, and in spite of the interruptions. I would like to be able to get to 250 pages. After that, we'll see.

> With best wishes,
> Raymond

OK, I'll leave this here, and we'll see. Now perhaps I should tell about my mother's family.

I don't know much about my mother's origin. And even less about my father's.

About my father I know that he was born in March 1904, in Siedlec, a little town in Poland near the Russian border. That's what is indicated on the *Acte de Disparition* I obtained after the war from *Le Ministère des Anciens Combattants et Victimes de Guerre* when I searched the archives to find out what had happened to my parents. On that document his first name is given as *Szama,* his Polish name. But in France everybody called him Simon. The Act of Disappearance does not indicate the day of his birth. Only the month. I know that my father had three brothers and five sisters. Most of them died in concentration camps. I never knew my grand-parents who lived and died in Poland. Those are the only facts I know about my father and his family.

As for my mother, this is what I learned from *L'Extrait des Minutes des Actes de Naissance du 5ème Arrondissement de Paris, année 1902.* I want to quote exactly what is written by hand on this old yellowed, half-torn document that I found in the box of papers and photos abandoned in the bedroom closet of our apartment in Montrouge.

> *Le dix septembre mil neuf cent deux, à une heure du soir, est née, dans le domicile de ses parents, rue Saint-Séverin 8, Marguerite, du sexe féminin, fille de Salomon Epstein, âgé de vint-sept ans, cordonnier, et de Rose Varseldorf, son épouse, âgée de trente-et-un ans, ménagère. Mariée à Paris, 4ème arrondissement, le ving-huit janvier mil neuf cent ving-six, avec Szama Federman.*
>
> *Pour extrait conforme*
> *Paris, le cinq décembre mil neuf cent quarante-et-un*

Here is a literal translation of that birth certificate.

> On the 10th of September 1902, at 1:00 in the evening, was born, in the home of her parents, 8 rue Saint-Severin, Marguerite, of the feminine sex, daughter of Salomon Eptstein, 27 years old, shoemaker, and of Rose Warseldorf, his wife, 32 years old, a homemaker. Married in Paris, 4th Arrondissement, on the 28th of January 1926, with Szama Federman.

Conform extract
Paris, December 5th 1941

It's all there. That's how one reduces the essential facts of a person's life to a paragraph.

One almost feels like laughing or crying reading such a document. What style!

But from this birth certificate I did learn a number of things I didn't know before—the address where my grandparents lived, that my mother was of the feminine sex, that my grandfather was a shoemaker four years younger than my grandmother, and that my mother and father were married on the 28th of January, 1926.

I have no idea why my mother needed this birth certificate in 1941. Probably to prove that she was a French citizen. That was the time when Jews had to declare their identity, and wear the yellow star.

My mother had five sisters and two brothers. Here is the list in chronological order of the Epstein children.

Fanny
Jean
Marie
Léa
Marguerite
Maurice
Rachel
Sarah

Except for Marguerite, my mother, all her sisters and brothers died in their own beds of old age. My mother was thirty-nine when she was ...

Federman, these details about the origin of your parents are interesting, but a bit sad. Do you think they are necessary?

It's especially my mother's birth certificate that I wanted to include here. The style and the tone of these documents are so laughable. It adds a touch of humor to the sadness.

I always imagined that my maternal grandparents were Polish. But one day, after the war, talking with my aunt Fanny, I asked her where my grandparents lived in Poland, and she said to me, Oh, no, my mother and father were not Polish. They were Palestinians.

Palestinians!

Yes, we are Palestinian Jews, she explained. There were many Jews in Palestine during the 19th century. Your uncle Jean and I were born there. But you won't believe this, my aunt said, at a moment when things were not going well in Palestine, the whole family moved to Poland. Don't ask me why. It was such a crazy idea. Marie and Lea were born in Poland. But life in Poland was worse than in Palestine because of the pogroms. So around 1900, your grandparents emigrated to France with four children. Your mother, Margot, was the first to be born in France, and then three more children after that, Maurice, Rachel, and Sarah.

Everybody called my mother Margot. So being French born, she was a French citizen. That's what the birth certificate indicates.

I suppose that means that I am of Palestinian origin, at least on my mother's side. That's why I've always been fascinated by the desert. I have a passion for the desert. I feel that I am a nomad. When I was a child, I dreamt of wandering in the Sahara with the Foreign Legion.

I should perhaps say more about my mother's brothers and sisters. After all, they were all present during my childhood. I would see my aunts and uncles and cousins when the whole family gathered on

Sunday at my grand-mother's apartment. So without elaborating too much, this is what I can recall about them.

My aunt Fanny was married to Nathan Gotinsky. They didn't have children. They sold kitchen utensils at the *marché*. They had a little truck. They were well to do, but they lived in a very small apartment in the *14ème arrondissement,* not far from where my grand-mother lived. I liked my aunt Fanny. She was nice to me and my sisters. When we went to visit her, she would slip a little money to my mother without Nathan noticing. Nathan was totally bald, with yellowish skin, and a lot of freckles on his face. He only spoke Yiddish to me even though I didn't understand what he was saying. He always insisted on playing cards with me. Belote. I usually won. He was not very smart. Fanny was the boss in that family. After the war, Nathan finished his life in Charenton, the famous insane asylum of Paris.

Ida was the wife of my uncle Jean. They lived in the suburbs. I don't remember which one. We didn't see them often. Jean worked in a factory, so he was not rich. Ida and Jean had a daughter, Renée, whom I never really knew well. When my aunt Ida died rather young, Jean remarried a woman who was not Jewish. After that he rarely visited my grandmother and the rest of the family, and when he did, he always came alone. My grandmother and the rest of the family were angry with him for having married a *shikse*. I believe that when the Jews started to be deported, Jean and his daughter spent the rest of the war hidden at his wife's parents farm. I cannot remember her name, but I liked her. She had a good farm woman face. She was always smiling, and when we visited her, she would bake special cakes for us. After the war I lost contact with my uncle Jean and his wife. And also with my cousin Renée.

The next in age was my aunt Marie. She had married Leon Marcowski the tailor. They had one son, my cousin Salomon. I knew them best since we all lived in the same apartment building. They were the wealthiest of the aunts and uncles, and aunt Marie thought of herself as the matriarch of the family. She was the one who organized the Sunday lunches at my grandmother's, and decided who should come on such and such Sunday. Not all the aunts and uncles came at the same time because grandmother's apartment was very small. And besides they didn't get along with each other. My mother and her three children were invited every Sunday. That's because we were poor, so this way we would eat well that day. My father never went with us.

I don't remember Lea's husband, but their family name was Abramowitz. We rarely saw them. They lived in Montreuil in a fancy apartment. They were very *embourgeoisés*. They owned a large shoe store. During my entire childhood we visited them only three or four times. They had one daughter, Agnes. A little snob who thought of herself a *grosse merde* because her parents were rich. And she acted like she was beautiful. When she was still very young, she would wear red lipstick, and red nail polish. Personally, I didn't find her very attractive. When she and her parents came to the Sunday lunch at my grandmother's, she was always trying to attract attention to herself. My sisters and I never played with her. She was older than us. Her parents would get into arguments with the other aunts and uncles. Usually about money. I saw my aunt Lea and my cousin Agnes only once after the war.

Maurice's wife was called Jeannette, but everybody called her Nenette. She was blonde. Everybody in the family loved her. I say the wife of Maurice, but in fact, they were never married, though they lived together. Nenette was Catholic. The reason she was accepted in the family was because, unlike Jean and his Catholic wife, Maurice and Nenette never married. So in the mind of my grandmother, that did not affect her Jewish religious belief. She thought that Maurice and Nenette had not married out of respect for her. But not so Jean. When I was a boy I never understood why Nenette could come to the family gatherings and not Jean's wife.

Maurice and Nenette didn't have children. They also owned a truck and sold toys at the *marché*. On Sundays when they came for lunch they would always give little toys to the grandchildren, either a yo-yo, or a jump rope, or a spinning top, or a game. The toys would occupy us while the grown-ups sat around the table drinking hot tea in glasses with pieces of lemon floating on top. Unfortunately for me, my uncle Maurice did not sell tin soldiers.

I never knew my aunt Rachel during my childhood. As I've told in **Aunt Rachel's Fur**, she escaped at the age of fourteen from the orphanage where she was with my mother. For many years she lived in the French colonies, in Asia and Africa. So I cannot say anything about her in relation to my childhood, except that she sent money regularly to my grandmother. All the aunts were saying that she was a dancer. But Leon kept saying that she was a prostitute.

I met her for the first time after the war when she came to France for a few weeks to see if her brothers and sisters had escaped deportation. At that time she was living in Senegal where she owned two hotels in Dakar. When I first saw her, I was struck by her resemblance to my mother, only much prettier. During her stay in Paris, she was very nice to me and generous. She would buy me things. My first wristwatch. She also had a suit made for me, not by Leon, but by one of the tailors on the *grands boulevards*. Everyone in the family wondered how rich she was because she spent money so freely. She wore a lot of make-up on her face, and even false eyelashes. She had expensive clothes, including an elegant fur coat. I became very fond of her, and she of me. I was only sixteen then. She would take me dancing in night-clubs. She wanted me to come with her to Senegal. She would say to me, You'll have a good life there in my hotels, I'll take care of you. I was sixteen then and so romantic. I had just returned to Paris from three miserable years on the farm. I was confused. I didn't know what to do. I think she thought of herself as a replacement for my mother. Though I was tempted to go with her to Senegal, and live a wild adventure, instead I went to America, to live a different adventure. So far as I know, she was never married and never had children. When Senegal became an independent country, she sold her hotels and she moved to Paris, where she died at the age of seventy-seven. She left all her money to the orphanage where she and my mother and her brother Maurice were raised. I thought it was a beautiful gesture. Her sisters and brothers were furious with her for having done that.

I don't remember my aunt Sarah's husband. I was still very young when he abandoned her and their daughter Solange, who was less than a year old then. Solange was the youngest of all the grandchildren. After she was deserted, Aunt Sarah lived alone her entire life, whining all the time and depending on her brothers and sisters for support. My cousin Solange was very cute. I liked her, but she was too young to play games with us when we saw her. Solange now lives in Ivory Coast. She married an African whom she met when he was studying in France. I admire her a great deal for having had the courage to escape from a mother who was stifling her with attention rather than affection. She did well in Ivory Coast. Her daughter Animata is a doctor in Abidjean, and her son Alain a pilot for Air Africa. When it was known that Solange had married a black man, her mother and the rest of the family rejected her completely, and even refused to see her children. A few years ago I went to visit my cousin Solange and her husband Johnny in Ivory Coast. I found a woman of great beauty and courage of whom I am very proud.

Well, that's it for the family on my mother's side. Except for my mother who had three children, it was a rather sterile family. Only four cousins, from seven brothers and sisters.

On my father's side three of his sisters and one brother lived in Paris. I've written quite a bit about them in my other books. Especially in **To Whom it May Concern.** So no need to tell more. The rest of my father's family who stayed in Poland all died in the concentration camps. They ...

Federman, tell the truth. The reason you're constantly referring to your other books is to have your readers buy these. A clever way of self-advertisement.

No, that's not the reason. It's to avoid repeating what I've already told elsewhere. Otherwise, I'll be accused of self-plagiarism.

But enough about the family. Now I want to tell something about my sisters.

I've never succeeded in writing much about my sisters, except for their names which I often repeat.

I have only one photo of me with my sisters. The photo I found in the small box in the bedroom closet. It's from this photo that I can say something about them. I have no other real memories of our playing together, or arguing as children always do.

I don't usually like to look at old photographs. They are supposed to show a real moment, but in fact they falsify that moment. Photos are fabricated objects. The photo I have of the three of us looks like it was taken by a professional photographer who had no idea who we were. But I like looking at it.

It is difficult to say how old we were at that time. I'll guess Sarah was about nine, Jacqueline five. There were four years' difference between them. Me, I was exactly in the middle. Two years younger than Sarah, and two years older than Jacqueline. In the photo I am also between my two sisters. That's how I remember them, always one to each side of me, as if they wanted to protect me. Though they have been absent for more than sixty years, even today I feel their presence. And yet, I have never been able to write anything of substance about them. I only remember a few words that passed between us.

I was half asleep that July morning when I saw my sisters for the last time. From behind the door of the closet, I heard them go down the stairs. In my head I have a blurry image of them. But in the photo I see them clearly.

It's a black-and-white photo. A bit yellowed now. My sisters are both wearing dresses. Sarah's hair is short. Jacqueline's is long and curly. Jacqueline is smiling. Sarah has a more severe smile. Me, I am wearing a jacket and a beret. I am smiling more than my sisters. There is nothing behind us. We must have been posing in front of a wall or a curtain when this photo was taken, probably in the photographer's studio for a special occasion. I don't remember. But that must have been why we were wearing our nice clothes. I wonder how my mother paid for this occasion.

It is difficult to make out the color of my sister's hair and eyes. I believe Sarah's hair was black, Jacqueline's brownish. Sarah resembled my mother. Jacqueline looked more like my father. So Sarah must have had dark eyes too like those of Maman, and Jacqueline grey eyes like Papa's. Mine are dark like Maman's.

Every time I look at this picture, a scene from our childhood comes to me. Especially when I look at Jacqueline. A distant moment engraved in my mind. It was the day when Jacqueline and I were playing doctor. I often replay that scene.

It was the end of summer 1939. September 3rd to be exact. The day France declared war on Germany. That day my sisters and I were on vacation on a farm, sent there by the city of Montrouge. Every summer, schools would select children of poor families to be sent on vacation for two weeks. Not to the *Côte D'azur,* but to some remote corner of the countryside so that the poor children would not bother the rich children who were sunbathing and swimming in the Mediterranean.

Toward the end of that summer, a group of children were sent, to a little village of the *Poitou*. The children were lodged on different farms for the two weeks of vacation. There was always lots of food on farms. And we were able to help with simple chores. Like feeding the animals.

I'll skip the description of the farm. It was just a typical French farm of the period. An old dilapidated farm house, a dark and dusty barn, lots of domestic animals, cows, horses, pigs, chickens, rabbits, and lots of manure. Two old tires were hanging from a tree for the children to swing on. Behind the farm house there was a meadow next to a little stream where the children could go wading.

As for the weather, on that memorable day, let's say hot and humid. The scene I remember vividly takes place in the barn. Old rusty farm tools everywhere. In a corner of the barn there is a huge pile of hay. The big double door is open. There are a few cows on one side of the barn tied with chains behind mangers. One can hear the noise of the chains clanking around their necks, and the sound of their mastication as they ruminate. One also hears the noise of the cow-dungs falling on the straw. In another corner of the barn two horses are sniffling and farting. There is dust in suspension in the sun rays that filter through the planks of the walls. But in spite of the heat and humidity, a nice day, and ...

Federman, you said you would skip the description of the farm, and here you are doing ultra-realism.

I'm not doing realism, I'm just staging the scene I'm going to relate. I know that descriptions are boring, but from time to time they are necessary. Otherwise you're going to say that what I'm writing is not fiction. So I'm describing the decor.

And now Federman takes himself for a theater director. Well, well.

To tell a story always demands some staging, and this one is like a little drama.

So, I continue.

In spite of the heat and the humidity, this farm is an ideal setting for a vacation. All the children are outside playing, some on the swings, others running around in the meadow, some plucking wild berries along the hedgerows, others chasing the chickens in the farm yard or climbing up the trees.

Raymond and Jacqueline are not outside with the other children, they are playing in the barn. The game they are playing must be funny because one can hear them chuckle. They are playing doctor. Raymond is the doctor examining the anatomy of his little sister. They are both laughing happily. Jacqueline is eight years old, Raymond ten.

Their sister Sarah is not playing with them. She is not in this scene. She will be later. And also their mother. Sarah thinks of herself too grown up to play with them. Especially your stupid games, she tells them. She is sitting in the shadow of a tree reading. She's always reading books she never shows to her brother and sister. Today, if she was still alive, she would certainly be a poet.

So Raymond and Jacqueline are playing doctor in the barn when, after a long journey from Montrouge, their mother arrives in the late afternoon. When she learned that war had been declared, she immediately left to take her children home. Maman was a real *mère poule* always protecting her little chicks. Especially her little *poussin* Raymond.

Before going on, I must make a correction concerning the date. The scene I am describing did not take place the day war was declared, but the next day, because Maman could not have traveled from Paris to the farm in *le Poitou* the very day war was declared.

The French declared war on Germany at 5:00 p.m. September 3rd. I know this because once I had to verify the exact date and time for something I was writing.

Because the war was declared so late in the day, Maman must have come to fetch us the next day to bring us home, where Papa was waiting. She was worried. She wanted to protect us.

It must have taken her almost a full day to come from Montrouge because first she would have had to catch a train and travel for several hours from Paris to Poitiers, then take a bus to the little village near where the farm was located, and then walk to the farm, and ...

Federman, you would do anything to delay telling us what happened that day with you sister. Are you ashamed to tell us?

No, I'm not ashamed. Besides, I'm not going to go into the details of what Raymond and Jacqueline were doing. I simply want to say as much as possible about my sisters. So I'm adding details to make this moment with my sisters last longer.

I don't remember the name of the village, but it's not important. In any case, I am sure now that what I am about to tell happened on September 4th. The day after the declaration of war.

So here is Maman arriving at the farm late in the afternoon after a long journey. Still breathing heavily from the long walk on a dirt road from the village to the farm, she worriedly asks the farm lady where her children are. The farm lady tells her that the two young ones are playing in the barn with the cows. They love the animals so much. The older one is so serious. She must be somewhere reading a book. She loves to read. She'll surely be a school teacher when she grows up.

As I already indicated, the door of the barn is open. In the semi-darkness one can barely see the cows and the horses. The dust is still whirling in the fading sun rays. Jacqueline is lying on the hay in a dark corner of the barn, her skirt pulled up. She is being examined by Doctor Raymond. Jacqueline is chuckling gently.

Outside one can hear the noise of the children chasing the chickens in the farm yard.

Suddenly Maman appears in the entrance of the barn looking intensely into the darkness. She calls out, Raymond! Jacqueline! Are you in there, children?

Raymond and Jacqueline jump to their feet and together, with a voice full of surprise and apprehension they call back, Yes, we're here, and they emerge from the corner where they were playing brushing the hay from their clothes.

238

—What were you doing there? Maman asks.

—Nothing. We were just playing a game, Raymond and Jacqueline answer.

—What kind of game?

—We were looking for something in the hay.

—What sort of something?

—A little thing Jacqueline lost, Raymond explains.

—What little thing?

Suddenly Sarah appears in the barn. She's now in the scene. With an ugly sneer, she points to Raymond and Jacqueline, and says, They were playing doctor. Raymond was playing with Jacqueline's little thing.

Raymond and Jacqueline are trembling with fear. But Maman doesn't scold them. She says nothing. Then she puts her arms around the three children. There are tears in her eyes when she says, We are at war. I'm taking you home. Papa is waiting for us.

We are at war, she repeats, holding us tighter in her arms. Then she lets go of us and tells us to get our things. We can still catch the bus and the last train to Paris. Maman is not crying any more. She's ...

Federman, so you were already a little pervert when you were a boy. Weren't you ashamed to play with your sister's thing?

Not really. All little boys want to know what little girls hide under their skirts. And I am sure all little girls also want to know what is hiding inside little boys' pants. It's normal.

Federman, nothing is normal with you. Maybe your sister didn't like what you were doing to her. Maybe she felt you were imposing yourself.

I don't know what my sister was thinking or feeling, but she was laughing. Perhaps she was feeling what William Butler Yeats expressed so beautifully in his poem "Leda and the Swan," the shudder in the loins.

My sisters never knew le frisson au bas du ventre. *It was denied to them. Unless they were ... Oh, what a horrible thought.*

You could have told something else. Another story of what you did with your sisters.

Tell what? The sordid moments we spent together in our crummy little apartment in Montrouge? That would reduce the story of my sisters to pathetic naturalism. My sisters deserve better than that.

But what I'll insert here is the poem I wrote for my sister Jacqueline.

OUR SISTER

in memory

Brother, she says,
from far away in the dark
write the poem
I will whisper to you,

but he is afraid
that the words
will not come out right.

Brother, she says, her voice rising
from a little pile of ashes,
when you crossed the ocean
and felt sick to your stomach,
did you feel sick for me too?

Brother, she says, among dead leaves,
when you fell in love the first time
and felt the great original *frisson*
and everything in you was giddy,
did you also feel happy for me?

I wish I could say more about my sisters, but that's all that's left of them – that photo, and Maman squeezing us in her arms when war was declared.

This morning, as I reread what I have already written about my childhood, I realize that the story is finished.

I had promised to tell the most important moments of my childhood. I don't think there is much more to tell. What could be told would be what usually happens during any childhood, happy and unhappy moments.

Besides, just as my childhood was brusquely interrupted the day my mother hid me in the closet, and I heard her last word. The story of my childhood should also stop abruptly.

But I would still like to tell one happy moment with my mother which I have never forgotten.

It was on my birthday. I don't remember which one. I had gone to the bakery with my mother. When she was ready to pay for the bread she was buying, she said to the *boulangère, Donnez-moi aussi un éclair au chocolat.* It surprised me that my mother was buying only one éclair.

In the street my mother gave me the éclair and said, Here, for your birthday, but eat it now, and don't tell your sisters.

My poor mother that day could not afford to buy three chocolate eclairs for her children.

This book is for my mother.

244

Federman ...

Yes? What?

Nothing ...

246

Shhh...Chut

Afterword

As Federman Used to Say

by Ted Pelton

As Federman used to say when I was his student in the mid-80s that each of his books began with a sentence he heard in his head, here is a sentence for Federman, who recently, as he would also say, changed tense—a death sentence if you will, for Raymond, who was himself both fact and fiction, so that it was difficult to tell which was which, as he was French, but also American, had been a US citizen from before I was born, had fought in the Korean War and jumped out of airplanes in an American army uniform, and yet whose accent sounded so f.o.b. that you didn't at first take note of the dissonance it created with his superb facility with the English language, and who would himself downplay that facility because, as he once also told me, he was not interested in belles lettres but instead, Pelton, he would say, I want to write *lettres de merde,* adding the translation immediately afterward, *I want to write shit letters, Pelton,* and now I cannot even think of him speaking to me in those days without hearing in my head him calling me not Ted but then always *Pelton,* thickly French-accented, so that it rhymes with *Bell-tone,* and which I'm not sure he even did all that often, it was a long time ago, and this was always one of the points of Raymond's writing, that there is no getting back to what actually happened because we confuse it with our stories and our stories become layers of sediment over the originary moment which, when we look for it, isn't there, or is underneath, or of changed contour, or is not really of interest anyway because what has come later, what has replaced it, what has become the memory stand-in, the usurper, the that-which-if-you-didn't-know-better-you-would-swear-was-the-memory, a process I was already aware of in Ray's work, but which was revealed to me just this past year as even more radically at issue than I had supposed when I was speaking to his daughter Simone and I recalled in passing the "closet episode," the originary moment of the creation of the Federman we all know, when he was cut off from all that he was theretofore and entrapped like a bug in amber in history and accident when the French police in league with the Gestapo came up the stairs to his family's apartment and his mother said *Shhh* and pushed him in the closet and the rest of the family was deported to Auschwitz, and Simone said, *Yeah, if that's really what happened*, because with Federman one finally can never be completely sure, everything is up for grabs, even as his work grounded itself in that which was so horribly, unspeakably factual, six million times factual, nine million times factual, so factual that to deny its facticity is a criminal offense in many parts of the world, but that even so, finally, like all else, becomes words, became words, changed tense, as Raymond himself now has, kept from doing so for sixty-seven years by the actions of his mother in his story, the mother to whom he dedicates the final words of his final book in English, that the press I direct, Starcherone Books, has now published—"This book is for my mother / Federman? / Yes? What? / Nothing...."—so that, of course, it is unsatisfying to call this just a story, of course, that which relates to life and death, or to the saving of a life, or to a new birth, or to a first birth, of course, this is not merely story, or rather, mere and story should not be linked together, and, of course, accidents happen, because mere in French is mother, *mère*, of course we should not make light, we should not pun and, of course, this is what *The Voice in the Closet* is also all about, the travesty of taking experience and making it into story, and I quote, *no I cannot resign myself to being the inventory of his miscalculations I am not ready for his summation nor do I wish to participate any longer willy nilly in the fiasco of his fabrication failed account of my survival abandoned in the dark with nothing but my own excrement to play with now neatly packaged on the roof to become the symbol of my origin in the wordshit of his fabulation,* unquote, of course, there is a real, and of course the story cheats it of its power, falsifies it in representing it, misrepresents it, of course, but you can still tell this story Raymond, they would tell him, it's a great story, of war and its aftermath, of loss and individual courage and carrying on, of coming to the land of opportunity, why do you insist on messing it up with all that trivia, of course it's interesting theoretically, they would tell him, but what our readers really want is the story, so why don't you just get rid of all that stuff about the noodles and the apartment and the trivia and the toothpaste and your car and masturbation, and of course it can't really be told, they would tell him, but that's the business of writing, it's entertainment, we all know that, of course what happened to your family is terrible, awful beyond words—people want to hear that story, and they want to hear about the young man who came to America and became a success, that's the best kind of story, tell that, they would tell him, you will make a lot of money... and Federman said, and those of us who love him love him for this, You know, Ted, for he was calling me Ted by this time, we had become friends, it was many years later, You know, Ted, I went home and I locked myself in a room and I spent two years demolishing that novel, I wrecked it, I took their notion of coherence and dismantled it, I threw words and letters all over the page, I dismembered that novel, I destroyed it, I massacred it, I decapitated it, and it became words, and fragments of words, and pictures and designs made out of letters on the page, and I never made a penny, because it became words and letters and incoherence and I would not tell their story, because I told the only stories I could tell, and there is no distinction between memory and imagination, I would not falsify, because I would not lie, because when I walk down the street, my sisters might turn the corner ahead of me and meet me there, and I have to believe that, and how could I tell them when I saw them that I had lied, that I had taken the money, that I had sold them for coin, that I had pissed on their memory, that I had not insisted on the truth in my fictions?

Also available from Starcherone Books

Kenneth Bernard, *The Man in the Stretcher: previously uncollected stories*
Donald Breckenridge, *You Are Here*
Joshua Cohen, *A Heaven of Others*, illustrated by Michael Hafftka
Peter Conners, ed., *PP/FF: An Anthology*
Jeffrey DeShell, *Peter: An (A)Historical Romance*
Nicolette deCsipkay, *Black Umbrella Stories*, illustrated by Francesca de Csipkay
Raymond Federman, *My Body in Nine Parts*, with photographs by Steve Murez
Raymond Federman, *The Voice in the Closet*
Raymond Federman and **George Chambers**, *The Twilight of the Bums*, with cartoon
    accompaniment by T. Motley
Sara Greenslit, *The Blue of Her Body*
Johannes Göransson, *Dear Ra: A Story in Flinches*
Joshua Harmon, *Quinnehtukqut*
Harold Jaffe, *Beyond the Techno-Cave: A Guerrilla Writer's Guide to Post-Millennial Culture*
Janet Mitchell, *The Creepy Girl and other stories*
Aimee Parkison, *Woman with Dark Horses: Stories*
Ted Pelton, *Endorsed by Jack Chapeau 2 an even greater extent*
Leslie Scalapino, *Floats Horse-Floats or Horse-Flows*
Nina Shope, *Hangings: Three Novellas*

Purchase through
www.starcherone.com, www.spdbooks.org, or www.amazon.com
or
Starcherone Books, PO Box 303, Buffalo, NY 14201

Starcherone Books is a signatory to the Book Industry Treatise on Responsible Paper Use and uses postconsumer recycled fiber paper in our books.

Starcherone Books, Inc., is a 501(c)(3) non-profit whose mission is to stimulate public interest in works of innovative fiction. In addition to encouraging the growth of amateur and professional authors and their audiences, Starcherone seeks to educate the public in self-publishing and encourage the growth of other small presses. Information about our submissions policies, donations, and ordering, as well as free samples of our authors' works, may be found at www.starcherone.com.